Other Books by *S. J. Rivera* from **Broken Sword Publications**

Alcohol Soaked & Nicotine Stained (2002)

Demon in the Mirror (2007)

Broken Sword Publications

Amerikkkan Stories

Hardcore Poetry

S. J. Rivera

Broken Sword Publications

For Sofia & Kat

CONTENTS

Preface: A Stranger in a Strange Land

I. Bullets, Bibles & Other Tales of Amerikkkan Justice

II. Gun Powder, Psalms & Shrapnel

III. Amerikkkan Stories

Preface: A Stranger in a Strange Land

When I started writing this book I was working as an Emergency Medical Technician on the streets of Jacksonville, Florida. Originally, I intended to write this book about my experience on the ambulance but in its creation it has become much more than that. Northeast Florida is more than the sum of its parts, as are these so-called United Sates of America and so this book has become a collection of experiences.

This particular assemblage of work was created from 2007 to 2011. Some of what you read here stems directly from my EMS experience but much more than that, from my experience as an Amerikkkan observer living in uncertain times. It relates my experience as a Chicano writer moving to and living in the storied and sometimes turbulent South.

I am but a stranger in a strange land and these are not only my stories, they are also yours. Living in a place completely disconnected from almost everything that made me whole can have a profound effect. To say the least, I am still walking the invisible line between two cultures.

There are many tales here - some of them are local and many of them are quite dark. Others are an attempt to reach out from behind state lines, back to a past I left behind, looking for some kind of rekindled self-identity. Still, other stories are present here so that I can speak at the frontlines of battles I would not otherwise see in the flesh – this new culture war.

If I have discovered one thing putting this book together it is that poetry does not extinguish the fires of the world. Poetry does not stop bullets. It does not serve as a tourniquet for the bleeding.

Poetry, by no fault of its own, creates a footnote in time for later reflection, when the storm has passed and the bleeding stopped…and sometimes that's enough.

If anything, this book is a record of what went down these last few years where the world tipped upside down and everything slid backwards.

If you are reading this I am thankful and hope that this book serves as something you can turn to for truth, inspiration or solace during these dark days.

This book encompasses many journeys – both to the past as well as to the present and beyond. Some of these stories are deeply personal and some are just for the sake of poetry but all of them are uniquely Amerikkkan.

This book is a labor of love and also of loathing. We live in strange times to say the least. I am not sure historians will look kindly upon this period but I write to remember it because we live in the instantaneous and in the hypereal - I write lest I forget and move on to the next best/worst thing as so many of us do.

Lastly, reader, I think that in some of these stories I have been searching for something tangible to grant me a sense of identity in a place where I have none other than my own bloodline and the reflection in the mirror. It is my hope that you may find a piece of yourself within these pages when you need it. These are all little stories, each of them their own universe and I have enjoyed writing them and hope you will enjoy reading them.

Thank you for reading.

SJR 5.30.11 Saint Augustine, Florida

Bullets, Bibles & Other Tales of Amerikkkan Justice

Drive-By on the Wrong Side of Town

There's no one out at four in the morning

the streets are empty and all I ever want to do

is crawl back into bed and pretend that the world is not ending

one person at a time

it's like driving through a haze of smoke

with cops and whores basking in the glow

of harshly colored streetlights and cigarette cherries

malt liquor bottles and shoes hanging from a high tension wire as

I roll down the street and look back at the faces

looking at me with bad intentions

where warriors stare down their own reflections on the tinted glass

as we do our own drive-by

in this neighborhood

and light up the night sky once again

I know just as well as they do that we don't belong here

but we go anyway because that's the job

it becomes a cheap form of entertainment

on the nights when the dead are not doing their job

we are detached – mere spectators with blood on our gloved hands

and memories in our back pockets like cigarette burns

these streets make the headlines every morning

and every day I come back for more

fuck reality television

this is the news

Actionville

Here, you become:

a firefighter

a cop

a nurse

a statistic

here, you are taught:

to extinguish the flames

to protect and serve

to heal the sick and wounded

to be on the wrong side of the law

here, under the guise of a metropolis:

killing is the business and business is booming

blood flows freely through city streets

as a commodity not unlike crude oil

and the so-called media covets this red gold rush

here, where Florida begins:

the roles are clearly defined and the stage set

there is never a shortage of players

nor any hope for anything but the last curtain

the show must go on

and on

here

Where Florida Begins

What a strange goddamn city this is

from the prayers in city hall

to the hookers on Philips highway

the emptiness of the core

from Eureka Gardens to Ponte Vedra Beach

the stadium to Highway 301

if all you did was look at the beaches or

watch the surfers ride the waves rolling in

you would think this area rivaled Hawaii

never once knowing about the crack heads

in the abandoned apartments downtown

all the people shooting drugs into their blood or

the trailer parks where domestic abuse is a contact sport

with cheerleaders and referees

or the innumerable angry Black youths

killing each other on a nightly basis

in whole parts of town that lack a single bookstore

yet this is a surf town

a fishing village

the first coast

and the last in line

see you on the news

Nothing Good Happens After Midnight (Duval Saying)

You can talk to all the dead vets from the Ho Chi Minh trail

all of the burnt addicts and wasted junkies littered alongside city streets

ask anyone from the wrong side of the tracks here - the ones serenaded by

sirens and bathed in strobe light

you can ask them all and they will tell you the same thing:

shell shock is a hell of a drug

I am sitting in the truck behind the hospital

it's 3:00 in the morning - the witching hour

the crazies are still parading in and out of the ER door like some Hellish circus

a man with a steak knife sticking out of his chest leads the crowd

they are all here: the hookers, the crack heads, the victims, the boozers

the dopers and pushers, the vampires and the pigs

they all want a piece - they all smell blood

they are all waiting for their 15-minutes

I have vacant, bloodshot eyes and the drone of radio static filters in and out of

my brain as I watch everything unfold before me

the aluminum siding on a building catches the reflection from the helipad's

colored lights and I can hear the propeller's slow-motion chop

the war sirens wailing: Incoming!

wind-blown palm trees, Jim Morrison and bloodied body parts scattered

in my mind - just another trauma alert landing and I am in a daze

not really wanting to know what's coming

because nothing good happens after midnight

It's then that I realize

I still haven't washed the blood off of my shirt

Three Dollars and a Prayer

They stabbed a guy here for $3 yesterday

the paper said the kids who did it were looking for gas money

and answers to questions never asked

Action News shoves a microphone in the victim's face

they want to know how he feels

even as he bleeds to death in the middle of a busy intersection

where the people are too preoccupied with their phones and coffee to care

The family wants to know "why" and

the camera's eye turns to the audience

who has already changed the channel in search of the next fix

This all goes down on a daily basis

here where the cats prowl

where there are no bookstores to speak of

on the Black side of town

but there is lots of prayer to quell the masses

as their words of faith drip like molasses yet fail

to wash away the blood

City officials balk at progress

at relief

at grief

at anything other than a psalm

to restore the calm

among a city burning in flames and

drowning in ignorance

22

We all reap what we sow and when

suburbia no longer offers the protection of White flight

when the whole world is a ghetto

and not a soul can read the signpost up ahead

we will all say our prayers

as meaningless as the ones whispered now

meant to serve as some kind of tourniquet

to the bleeding

and as useful as a $3 bill

The Ballad of Richard Collier

During the Fall of 2008
in a quiet neighborhood near St. Vincent's hospital
the city of Actionville stood next to a mountain of a man
and chopped him down with the edge of its hand

Few had ever heard his name before
outside of the National Football League he was virtually unknown
until he suffered multiple gunshot wounds
while sitting in a car outside of an apartment building
late one night in the city where Florida begins

The holes in his body
created out of the stillness of an otherwise quiet Southern night
left him minus his career
minus two tree trunks for legs and
paralyzed from the waist down for the rest of his life
and then through the magic of television and ratings
everyone knew his name

14 bullets fired from a single firearm did this
expelled from a gun that could have been fired by the city itself
messages scrawled upon the bullets for all to witness
just as they do every Sunday morning

One bullet: for civic leaders with their heads buried in beach sand
One bullet: for a failed education system

One bullet: for another generation lost to violence

One bullet: for the blood flowing in to the St. Johns River

One bullet: for shooting first and asking questions later

One bullet: for an illiterate and angry population

One bullet: for daily homicide

One bullet: for closing libraries on the poor side of town

One bullet: for a city-wide lack of empathy and regional bigotry

One bullet: for all of the heartfelt prayers meant to solve real problems

One bullet: for the murder capital of Florida

One bullet: for the people who blame the victim for being out too late

One bullet: for the local media sensationalizing the violence to garner ratings

One bullet: for a city with an inferiority complex, a killing addition and an

invisible populace

Why Are You Watching?

I murdered my television with a twelve-gauge shotgun

I called it a sacrifice

I called it justice and then

someone called the police

After a few days of questioning and solitary confinement

they let me go

with the promise that I would

purchase another television set

and I did

bigger, better, more expensive than the last

with high definition and surround sound

I fell to my knees in divine worship

because no matter how many times I kill the fucking thing

I always crawl back to it on my knees

picking up the pieces and

begging for more programming as

I plug myself back in

It's all just a matter of wasted time and static

the church of the cathode ray cares not about your convictions

no amount of words can change that fact

I can dice it up any way I want to

here, there

in your crummy paper

or in a book

because everything looks the same in the ether and

shitty poetry will never do it justice

life is a series of mundane events and rituals

which you choose to take notice of is your own business

it may be only a finite number of times that you haul the trash to the curb

or watch a favorite TV show

and that's it

no amount of contrived nihilism changes the fact that

we all waste our lives on meaningless shit

trying to dull the agony of existence

with situation comedies and forensic dramas

and reality programming

the goddamned television will still be there

long after we are gone

waiting for the next species to make it God

The Fear Before A Moment of Protest

Why am I still nervous when a cop pulls up behind me in traffic?

I have done nothing wrong, there are no warrants

no all points bulletins floating my name in the airwaves

not even an unpaid parking ticket

yet I look into the rear view mirror and see hard eyes hidden

by mirrored sunglasses watching every move

punching names and numbers into the computer to see if it

spits out anything worthy of his attention

despite my legal status, all of my papers are in order

neatly tucked away in the glove box

the radio is not loud

my tires are normal

there are no empty beer bottles littering the floor of my suburban-friendly

vehicle so why the butterflies in my stomach?

I am unassuming and nonthreatening in every way but the hue of my skin

my children are with me, safely in their car seats

unaware of the sudden panic in my heart

I am a grown man and I have nothing to hide from the law except maybe

contempt and the kind of bitterness

evolved from a lifetime of mistrust

Pavlovian baton beatings from murderers with badges

who receive slaps on the wrist and the constant fear that I am but one

false move away from losing everything

in a moment of protest

Mayfield

Ward Cleaver:

the archetypal suburban father figure

was a philosophy major

which must have given him an insight to the art of parenting in black and white

Ward was also a veteran of the second world war

shell shocked and trigger happy whenever his wife would break a dish

Boom!

I sometimes imagine Ward Cleaver as an android

the thing is, Ward doesn't know he's an android, he just carries on until one day

Wally brings a Black girl home and Ward's circuits fry

his android face falls off revealing a menagerie of wires

and metal with wide-staring, artificial eyeballs

What then?

June would be a single mother

She would also become mentally unstable

she would be free from the tyranny of Ward

to pursue her passions and desires and

to ingest copious amounts of wine and Xanax

due to the realization that her former husband was a robot

and that she occasionally allowed him to penetrate her

when their beds were pushed together

she would also have the self-realization, as well as the fear

that she may also be an android but she would be too terrified to

find out for sure

The Neighborhood

When I drive past the confines of my comfortable subdivision
with its rows of well-kept homes
I see trailer park yards littered with the remnants of apathy
sun-bleached clothes strewn along hand-fashioned lines and the
half-dressed, haggard mothers
ears glued to cell phones, cigarettes dangling from their lips
pushing babies along the two-lane roads

I see battle flags illuminated by Friday night lights and
neon-lit crosses along neatly manicured lawns
where the sign in front of the church says: Jesus saves
there are abandoned homes with rotting vehicles out front
adorned with bitter political bumper stickers from years ago now
telling me to love it or leave it!

This is nowhere and this is everywhere: the crossroads
with a single flashing traffic light swinging in the wind
waiting on Satan to appear one night just down the road from the county jail
where they locked up a dream and prayed for salvation
they prayed for rain
they prayed for blood
they prayed for the ghosts of war to resurrect themselves
they prayed to avenge old scores
they prayed to the gods in the static ether to point out the heretics
they prayed to lynch people in the trees
they prayed for the end

Cancer

I wish I could cut my head open and extract all of the bad things

the way they do certain types of cancer

under the careful study of surgeons and sterile conditions

I'd scoop out pieces like an ice cream sundae

with a big spoon and an Exacto knife

careful not to drip any of the contents as I go

as it may burn holes through the floor and beyond

I am sure, with the right kind of eyes

you can look at your brain like some kind of twisted road map

every fucked up occurrence like a fork in the road

leaving its own scar like nicotine does to your lungs

I know that certain parts of my brain are blackened

like crude tar from the rage and gnashing of teeth

the purity of hatred

the lifetime of disappointment

the sickness of self-awareness and

the years of conditioning

I would cut all of it out if I could, keep those parts in a mason jar

hoping that I would heal into remission

instead of being eaten by parasites

that consume everything like wildfire

scorching all who stand in its path

leaving their ashes in the wake

like children scarred from watching parents

go after the throats of each other

with broken glass

The Demon in the Mirror

I am an angry, miserable mother-fucker when I look in the mirror
with only myself to blame
if I punched the reflection looking back at me
I would break through several sheets of glass
hearing the cacophony of laughter from generations past
because there is no family business
the only legacy I have before me is rage, abandonment
and silence disguised as pride
I never did anything heroic
I never did anything original
I never did anything that was not expected of me
and there was always a motive
assumptions from family, lies from Hollywood and
stereotypes from society at large
the constant whispers
the voices that only I can hear
when I lay my head on the pillow after
everyone else is asleep at night
these expectations end in the bottom half
of an electrical current running
from head to toe
with me grinning stupidly from ear to ear
as I peer into Hell through a jagged viewpoint
the hatred beckoning me and blood on my hands, no
wiser than before and definitely
not looking forward to what's next

The United

no one talks about the truth

    not politicians

    not the media

    no one

no one says:

    the united states of bullshit

    the united states of lies

no one says anything like that

no one walks up to a podium and says:

    you are all already dead

    everything is a lie

    now please buy more useless shit

    be fruitful and multiply

    take off your glasses and consume!

they refuse to acknowledge

    the united states of corporations

    the united states of bigots

    the united states of hypocrites

    the united states of sociopaths

    the united states of fences

    the united states of hatred

    the united states of neo-Nazis

no one says any of these things

because if they did

you would never hear from them again

I walked away

from uncles fighting

from little brothers crying

teen pregnancies

heroin addictions

infidelities and responsibilities

from fate and from iron bars and hate

from funerals for bad men

caring women dying in their beds

eaten alive by disease and hard luck in life

frail, bitter old men with drawers full of regret

birthdays, anniversaries, graduations, incarcerations

I walked away from it all and went to the beach instead

with cheap shades on and sunscreen

I let the ocean's waves drown out

the sound of cries for help

while I poured myself a drink

and let out a sign of relief

a drunk calm washing over me

letting my ignorance be bliss

out of sight

out of mind

until a decade later

when all I can think about is how

I walked away

The Seeds

Most of the things I thought were important once

mean little in the grand scheme of things, if such a scheme even exists

and I don't really believe one does

but you get my meaning

Why any of us feel the need to instill our own demons

into the minds of our children is beyond me

Some of the seeds get planted without even trying

but damn if we aren't all guilty of at least a little gardening.

We must all, on some level, hope to create more perfect versions

of ourselves; models without all the flaws and failures

yet that strategy never seems to work out very well, does it?

Why then do we try so hard to make it so?

Far too many of us look beyond the simple pleasures of

childhood and concentrate too much on expectations

when that harvest fails to produce

the relationship goes sour

What we say matters.

What we perceive and how we perceive it make an impact;

stronger than you could imagine.

Why then do some things stick and others do not?

Why do some seeds grow into poison

plants and strangle the rest of the garden?

No matter the past I hope to do the best job that I can

and enjoy it as much as possible.

I have always been one for living in the moment because,

to me, that's all we have.

Welcome to Dachau and Welcome to McDonald's

There's a McDonald's at Dachau

less than a mile from the actual concentration camp

where years ago they passed out leaflets that said:

"Welcome to Dachau

and welcome to McDonald's"

welcome to McRe-Education

welcome McGlobalization

welcome to the New McWorld Order

would you like fries with that?

The Nazis stood for conformity

they stood for world domination

they stood for sameness

they stood for loyalty and identity

with easily recognizable symbols

and the corporate indoctrination

of the youth

the golden arches at Dachau

flying their flag high

is full of mothers and small children

and teenagers in "American" designer clothes

who are all consuming fast food

amalgamating themselves into the Reich

of Ronald McDonald

and lovin' it

Low skilled immigrants work the counters and cook the meals

as everywhere else in the world, millions of people

do the same things

order the same products

wear the same clothes

and make the same people rich

they all salute the same flag

one nation, under conformity

with Happy Meals and Coke for all

carrying out what Hitler could not

through processed food and saturated fat

with concentrated sugar and high fructose corn syrup

instead of gas and firing squads

and none of it matters

And if we eat McDonald's hamburgers

and potatoes for 1,000 years

we will become taller

our skin will become white

and our hair will be blond

or so they say...

there's only one way to find out

White Man's Burden

I have a reoccurring dream; it's about the faceless White man

his perils, plight and his tribes who were native to this land

long ago, before they were conquered by invading hordes

bearing false gods and pestilence

the White tribes were spread far and wide and from sea to sea

the Red men crossed the ocean, came ashore to conquer, rape and take the land

in the name of the All Father

time passed and the White man lost many battles

his kind succumbed to disease, famine and death

much strife was put forth upon his people

their struggle is legendary and largely undocumented

the Red man spread like sickness across the nation

multiplying in numbers no one had ever even thought possible

soon, the White man was outnumbered and pushed out

into the land the Red man did not want

the White man was given waste

it was there that he tried to preserve what little culture he had left

it was a struggle - one that continues on

fast forward to now: the Red man owns the world

     he controls the wealth

     he controls the religion

     he controls the language

     he turns his back on the past

the White man is scarce

     and forgotten

Rotten Fruit

Every day after reading the news,

drinking my coffee and setting the remaining thoughts

from yesterday on fire

I watch them burn in the yard

like newspapers eaten by flames

shrinking and turning black

floating up into the air

where no one can read them anymore

I think about what some of those pages say

and the rotten fruit some of them have bore;

vast orchards overrun with insects and weeds

dead bodies and decaying ideas

it reminds me of sitting in high school

sociology class, my teacher in lust

heavy eye contact and ill-intended innuendos

watching the LA riots unfold on a closed-circuit television

with a loaded gun in my pocket

listening to uppity children from conservative backgrounds,

wax poetic about the "niggers" on TV

and how they are reducing their own neighborhood to ashes,

"Why don't they burn Beverly Hills?" one of them asks

the subterranean, suburban commentary on the fall of Rome

falls just short of a violent classroom soliloquy

because the hammer was cocked

there just wasn't enough nerve

there never is

Going Back Home Again

A million miles from anywhere, together
no calendar on the wall

no clock ticking
just moments guarded by golden-rusted memories

the waitress brings frosted pitchers of beer,
while we play yet another game of 8-ball

look at each other, wiser eyes against the green felt
fumbling to sink even the easiest of shots

because age has the better of any of us now
but the night carries on

I think if any of us had a choice
no one would ever leave that bar

after we pay the tab and
walk back out into the cold

we all shake hands because
that's what you're supposed to do

we know it's probably one of the last times
we will all ever see each other again before another 10 years passes by

Soy Ilegal

Since the beginning we, la raza odiada

the hated race

have been caught in the middle

just as we are now

between the fall of Tenochtitlan

and the migrant farms that feed a nation

in this modern day version of divide and conquer

1492

1942

2010

what's the fucking difference?

we are all just a bunch of savages

pachucos y wetbacks

soy ilegal

A flame to the codex

our history was/is destroyed by the original conquest

we have been fighting for our identity since Queen Isabella

ordered the rape of the land, the natives and the legacy

as we were oh so graciously pulled from the jungles

into modern day slavery

but you just call it industry

we may not have been brought across the ocean in ships

but we are in bondage just the same

hiding our tongue

afraid to give any clue about our identity

and so we have no identity

soy ilegal

I am neither here nor there

a wanderer without a motherland

the immigrant does not see me as brother

In Mexico I am a pocho

in the USA I am a dirty Mexican

the US Census says I am White

and to the voting population of Aryanzona I am the enemy

my whole life has been shadowed by the original struggle

always asking: *who am I?*

soy ilegal

I am tired of Mexican being a dirty word

I am tired of being told my history doesn't matter

I am tired of being an invisible pawn in an ancient chess game

you have taken my food

adopted my style

banned my language

and changed my name

the knife cuts deeper and the conquest stretches farther

yet we remain in defiance

this *is* American History X

and you shall not destroy it

soy ilegal

Freedom (for Leonard Peltier)

I read Leonard Peltier's book: Prison Writings

I did not understand the title until I learned what a Sun Dance ritual was

it is no surprise then that they did not destroy his will

but they gave it their best shot

I think about him once in a while

how one day in his life (the year after I was born)

his whole world changed

I think about Pine Ridge and the people there

the hard Indio faces that cameras always seem to catch

I think about how I am here listening to music

eating bad food and writing freely

he is still behind bars

rotting because of his associations, his defiance

and the color of his Red skin

nothing more, nothing less

he's been in there my whole life and it really doesn't matter to me

if he was at Pine Ridge or not

They only lock you up for that long [two consecutive life-terms]

because they know that eventually people will forget about you

and they do

when they locked up Leonard Peltier they were not just putting away one man

they were jailing an entire movement

too few people speak his name these days

it's the kind of thing that makes me feel quite old

and I am

Wasted Years

People I cared about once are dead now

that doesn't so much matter anymore

years passed without so much as a word between any of us

that is a strange way to pass the time

between friends and family

I remember how after a while

we all sort of forgot each other's faces

and we would laugh about it because

you would not think that was possible

there was always a simple connection that

no matter how long it had been since we last broke bread,

would bring us all back to the way it was before the long winter

the snow never melted after I walked away

things have a much different meaning now

bitter with frost and I am miles from anywhere

resembling home, years from the last supper

a death erases certain things in a similar fashion as

to how the evening tide creeps the sand back out to sea

the water here has run colder every year

and one of these days

I will have to start walking back home

before another 10 years slips through my fingers

Jesusland

They all look the same
I don't mean in a racial sense
I mean they have that "look"
They all look like they belong on the 700 club
"Stuffy" and "Prissy" doesn't quite do it justice
It's like Downs…only with a Jerry Falwell twist
these people need their own island

what life would be like for them should they collectively
pool their wealth, purchase their own private island
where they are all the same and free to live out Hitler's wet dream

I have asked many of them time and again:
what is it exactly that you all want?
"We want freedom got-dangit. And for you commie faggots
to git to France with all the other godless homos!"

They all want their own private Idaho
they can be free there
free from leftist persecution
no Blacks, no Gays, no Muslims
No Mexicans!
No liberals or commies, pinkos or anyone else
that pisses them off even slightly
No heathens
No science

No donuts

Just good old fashioned, god fearing 'Mericans

It will just be them

free to put "Christ" back in Christmas

free to salivate over the stockpile of guns and bibles

they can elect Rush and Sarah as their leaders

and for a time, it will be bliss

In a few short months

after failed attempts to start God's war

when they realize there is no one left to attack

they will let loose on each other like wild dogs

I suspect they will sodomize and cannibalize each other

in biblical fashion

while everyone else watches on pay per view

I Remember

I remember a lot of things

but I have forgotten much more than I care to admit

I remember a bunch of kids sitting around the kitchen table with tarnished

quarters and shot glasses

bitter vinegar wine and halfcocked bottles of MD 20/20

walking down the street in a blue button down flannel with a menthol cigarette

hanging from my lip

a bandanna tied tightly around my head

the bullet holes in the walls cannot say anything more but the train tracks across

the street still scream around 3 a.m.

I remember sitting on the porch drinking simple malt liquor and smoking until

dawn

sleeping until the afternoon only to tell more tall tales under the drunken

moonlight

the remnants of teenage drama so thick and love lives so sick and syrupy

I remember being lovesick and foolish

skipping work and cutting class

just to get my jealousy under control

I remember people I hardly knew as guests in my home and wanting to get away

from them

getting so drunk I had to sleep on the bathroom floor, locked inside

my face cool against the tile

backyard keg parties and front yard drive-bys in the summer heat
and the ominous alley way where lives were lost and hopes and dreams died

I remember staying up for days writing juvenile love letters to
the ungrateful and the immature ladies of the hour who loved to
devour the hearts of men for fun
not paying the bills and squandering food money on a music career
that went no further than the neighbors green shag-carpeted living room

I remember being alone on my birthday with no power and no savior
other than the pen in my hand and bitterness in my heart
thinking that there must be a better way but
settling for a cheap high and my mouth dry
only to succumb to my addictions again

Yeah, I remember a lot of shit
mostly I remember being young and free, naive mostly
free to do whatever I wanted, even take my own life inside of an old house
with dead memories and carpet so stained it remains there even now
telling stories to whoever will listen
but no one ever does
not even me

Hair of the Dog

Lloyd indulges my weakness at the bar

a little hair of the dog that bit me

sinking its teeth into my subconscious mind

and tearing it for all it's worth

wine, liquor and beer

just enough to satiate

just enough to hold it all back

just enough until I snap

I am not Jack Torrance.

       I am not Jack Torrance.

              I am not Jack Torrance.

                     I am not Jack Torrance.

       I am not Jack Torrance.

              I am not Jack Torrance.

I am not Jack Torrance.

       I am not Jack Torrance.

Yet I see myself in that photograph time after time, smiling

I know the look…

it's the same one I get when I drink

the alcohol stays in the blood for some time after

little demons floating through my veins

the anger is always early to rise and

a chemical transformation

performs a show if you watch the eye closely

Maybe there is something in the water

my head underneath the spigot

drawing in as much as I can take

slaking my thirst, my curiosity

my lust

maybe I have always been like this

as every man before me

something in the bloodline flowing

from one generation to the next

like slow poison coursing through

a history of violence [hidden]

just underneath the cool, suburban exterior

this thin layer of fat and fabric

behind the mask of forced smiles and backyard barbecues

[I am Jack Torrance]

calm, cool and collected

grinning and insatiable

writing the same sentence over and over

under this cool exterior

I am the caretaker

waiting to splinter a door into jagged pieces with an axe

unleash the demons that have waited

impatiently at the bottom of a bottle

…for far too goddamned long

Pride

I never felt like I could let my guard down, ever

like a pit bull that doesn't fight any longer

there is damage and I may lash out one day

for no reason

on someone who does not deserve it

where I come from you were always on edge

ready to prove something

it didn't matter what the reason was

I always walked tall

I never once looked away

and I've ground my teeth down all in anticipation

…of what?

I remember all of the crazy situations I used to get myself in the middle of

still proving a point

I have always placed myself in the middle, never taking a side

I stare into oncoming traffic

daring someone to hit me

but no one does

all the times I put myself in harm's way

just to say that I could

I put myself in the middle of gunfire

I shook hands with killers

I tempted fate and washed my hands

in the blood of the afflicted

I fled down the highway with a death wish

I tried to poison myself with substance (and a lack thereof)

I lit myself on fire and I shut myself off

I believed in absolutely nothing

I am still here

I am still trying to prove a point

I am still in the middle

I think I shall die with clenched teeth and bated breath

walking the prison yard inside of my mind

ever watchful of the guard towers and other sharks

roaming the endless waters

despite the fact that I have the key

I always have

I am my own worst enemy

Nightmare Soup

I've never been one to split my head open and share;

spill out all those nightmares and watch them wash down the gutter

like so much stale blood.

Not me.

Nope.

No reason to really.

The urge to spill my brains out all over the page

by the hand of an axe does not come too often these days,

mostly due to the repercussions.

I see myself in an empty bookstore,

talking about my body of work, staring at a sea of vacant seats.

The world is on fire outside and everyone is burning and screaming.

Not me. I'm inside talking to empty seats.

Outside I know that things are bad.

I can tell by the sirens and flashing lights, the constant screaming and mayhem

but I don't pay it any attention. I have a penitentiary in my mind that keeps all

of the dark shit locked up tight so as not to let a single drop spill out…most

nights anyway,

lest anyone see the roaches dripping in and out of my ears.

There are, of course, escapes sometimes.

Things get out.

Things that are beyond me.

Things I cannot control.

Things I try not to think about during the conscious hours.

I try and hunt them down as best as I can but sometimes they get away.

I wonder if I cut my head open

would you stick around to see what poured out?

Would it bother you?

Would you poke at it?

Would you catch it in a coffee can for safe keeping?

Only to open it up at a later date and have it crawl out

and raze the soul-called remnants of your life?

I can imagine you years from now opening up that coffee can,

dumping its contents into a sauce pan over medium heat.

I can see you laboring over it and stirring it with a wooden spoon.

Would it make good soup?

I cannot say.

It might surprise you though.

It might just be blood coming out of my head.

It might not.

It all depends on the lighting.

I suppose you'd have to stick around and see.

It could be all this black shit that I have holed up in there

would come pouring out and burn holes in the floor.

Maybe it would just spill down onto the ground and separate into thousands of

tiny insects

things you'd never want to know about all gushing out at once.

Nightmare soup.

Drowning Again

I'm floating out in the middle of the black ocean and sucking in water
and wind; waiting to fall to the bottom, waiting to fill my lungs
with more than they can handle.

I'm far off the coast and miles away from anything even resembling
civilization. I am surrounded by pieces of dead, burned and bloated flesh. The
wreckage is long gone. My ship has long sunk to the depths of the water and
there is no trace of it left to laugh at; just myself, floating there and waiting to
die like the rest of them.

Waiting to die makes you think of strange things. I've been reflecting
on obituaries that I have written. I am the epitaph man. I am the man who
writes the last words – I put the final words to their lives in print. I wonder who
will write mine? I suppose it doesn't really matter though I'd like to read it just
the same. What would they say? That I died a bitter man? A secretive old
bastard who held onto foolish dreams? I don't know.

The whole ordeal has made me consider the road home. I am floating
and dying and I caught up in cryptic sayings.

Things like: You can never go home again. That is a true statement.

There is no road. No map. No such person to point the way.

You really can't ever go home.

No matter how hard you try the walls still close up.

Brick by brick things are sealed off forever.

As soon as you step foot off of your native soil

the whole landscape changes behind you,

enveloping bits and pieces of your former self.

People forget your name.

Your memory grows stale.

You are forgotten.

You can never return home again, no, but you can certainly visit.

You can try and retrace your steps sometimes.

Sure, you can visit old places and seemingly familiar faces

but you know better.

Such visitation has the tendency to poison a person over time.

Rather than relive the past you are given sips of poison

to cloud your memory and remind you

that it was never as good as you thought it was and

that things are never, ever as good as you remember them to be.

I am thinking about the road back home

as massive sheets of water crash down on me

and make it hard to keep my breath for long.

The wind is freezing.

Every bit of the salt from the water hurts my skin and burns my eyes.

I know, deep down, that all I have to do is give up.

All I have to do is sink.

I know that if I let go all of it will go away and I can watch the scenery

from below as my lungs fill with salty and bitter water.

I know that if I drown myself maybe I can go home again,

maybe forever.

I can see the circling sharks beneath me.

I can see a lot of things beneath me.

Failures.

Mistakes.

Fuck ups.

Wrong turns.

Bitter family members.

Broken promises.

Everything I should have said.

Lies.

Faces in the murky water laughing at me

waiting for me to sink down to them so they can tear into me.

I can look down and see Hell waiting for me.

Maybe it's always been here.

Maybe it's been waiting for me to come down for a long time.

Maybe this is the final homecoming.

Flashes of lighting illuminate the water for just a second,

long enough to watch the predators moving about and waiting for me,

chewed flesh in their teeth, and their eyes without pupils or irises,

just milky white scleras and bitter grins.

I think maybe I will sink.

I think I will travel that road.

Just to test the waters.

Just this once to see what happens.

I think I want to go home again.

I think…

I've heard Hell is nice this time of the year.

By Any Means Necessary

A political drive-by, mother fucker

as you wait on the red light, feet tapping and eyes wandering

music floating in and out of your ear

you are unsuspecting, unassuming and then

bam! It hits you

By. Any. Means. Necessary.

I never thought I'd see the day when affluent, suburban teenagers

identify with rebellion by citing Malcolm X

to carry the causes of their parents down the road

pasted onto the backs of shiny Ford pick-ups

evoking the image of the man himself

poised in a moment on the brink of extinction

his finger on the trigger as he looks out the window at a future

he could never imagine

and yet here we are

Ward Cleaver has been mugged and left for dead

somewhere, someone is throwing up a flag

the light is green

The Way She Walks

The bar is filled with smoke, neon lights and the liquor-brave

sniffing for the scent of blood in the air, thick as thieves

the writing on the walls says: Attitudes gladly adjusted

the Cramps are playing: "The Way I Walk"

and among the mixture of broken glass and splintered chairs

she stands there on the stage, a menagerie

her eyes are closed and she's swaying her hips

in a punctuated shuffle, alone but definitely not unwatched

she is working herself into a melting frenzy

of sweat and heavy breathing

her writhing body form, damp with sweat

as her dress slowly makes its way up her thighs

so as to reveal a hint of garter with a pistol tucked inside

she rakes her hair back just as she parts her lips

tosses her head backwards and screams...

Aaaahuuuaa!!!!

a drunkard makes his way over to her and she smiles insidiously

with her lipstick smeared on her face

like bloodstains from a sacrificed lover

she grabs the turquoise from his necklace and kisses him softly

before biting his lip

and whispering into his hear

she sends him crashing to the floor with the heel of her boot

and shoots him in the face

Pieces

If I look ahead of me I see the barrel of a gun, looking back

only the charred remains of many yesterdays

a bullet in my head and Hell licking at my feet

there is no more running - I know that now

ten years of suppressed anger have found me

like an immigration raid long overdue

I am on the bus back to where

I should have always been

detained and deranged, ready

to be unleashed with a head full of furious ideas

and no one to understand the language

the shackles are thin and

when I do finally wash the blood from my hands

it will surprise no one, least of all

the man whose funeral I forgot or

the one who taught me how to kill

I have always been walking down this road, searching

for an exit sign along the way

weighing the borrowed time against

the alleged progress

even though fate was just another dirty word

I will succumb to it like a jealous lover

too blind to see what is ahead of me and too careless to look

after what I will leave behind

the pieces are no longer mine to pick up

Eulogy Prequel

It's the middle of the night and I am digging

my own grave with a rusty shovel.

My old man's old man is sitting there on top of the dirt.

He speaks to me in broken Spanish.

I tell him: I ought to be digging this hole for you

but he just laughs and tosses two coins down by my feet.

Dig, he says.

Dig, mijo.

I buried you long ago

in the deep recessive graveyard

at the back of my mind

along with all of the other bodies

rotting in unmarked holes

with overgrown vegetation and earth

covering their secrets and screams

their flesh and beauty eaten away from

years of rot and wear

with insects festering and multiplying

they remain mere bones and tufts of hair

an index of abandoned memories

with the caretaker long gone

dig, mijo, dig

Eulogy

You can see the heat rising off of the asphalt

born of the sun flowing down

warming the white concrete and turning black tar into

puddles flowing through gutters, the trees do not move

there is no wind, no sound, no quarter from the sun today

the wires on the withered telephone poles hum and

the street is pregnant with rows of seedy, neon-lit bars and

the carcasses of drunken fathers and husbands on the cracked walkways

a young boy makes his way into one of the bars

to ask for his estranged father

only to find him asleep and face down on the counter

these streets are worn with waste and death

these streets the boy's father walked and his father before him

these streets are blessed and cursed

their gutters filled with a mixture of broken dreams and blood stains

these streets I left behind with old ghosts and dead memories

the writing on the wall says: these men are departed

my father turns his back as we all follow suit this day,

we all run away until our lungs burn and legs fall numb

we never look back

for fear of seeing a reflection and getting sucked back in

and so we now lay you to rest old man,

where we will spend the rest of our days

trying to remember what you were not

The Fourth of July

There we are sipping warm beer under night skies

smoking cigarettes and listening to the jams on the radio

soothing sunburns and fragile egos with ice from the cooler and cheap liquor

waxing poetic about who got who's phone number and

balking at the embarrassment of rejection

there we are sitting on the grass

waiting for that special someone to call

the weather is warm and the fireworks give quick glimpses

of lovers, fighters and failures

it never mattered in the end

only the anticipation of the sun going down and

the light show to close the night out

illuminating the arguments in the parking lot

as a prelude to the long drive home

we all endlessly chattered about nothing in particular

some drunk, some sober

some left behind

the dreams still alive in our eyes

like the light of stars that burned out years ago

we carried the flames blindly into tomorrow

knowing nothing of the forgotten faces

the hearts broken or the memories lost

the casualties of another summer

there we are

The Sand

this feels like the desert

the emptiness

the uneasy quiet under a blood moon

with crawling sand underneath

the howling wind

carrying scant messages in the dusk

a faint echo of yourself

lost in this sea

obscure and murky

with far too many sharks looking to feast

I say your name

without a sound escaping

an airstream blasts it along

as a serpent

to nowhere and to nothing

I sink into fine granules

swallowed and silent

and disappear

This is Change?

A boy is murdered on the border

by heavily armed men in green uniforms

protecting an invisible line in the sand

and you smile

       this is an act of war by any other name

a little girl is murdered in her home

and you call them border activists instead

a Marine is murdered in his own home

by SWAT cops with the wrong address

and the media ignores it

in this day and age

where the word "Mexican" is itself pejorative

lies run rampant

as the words of a man who promised change

fall upon deaf and deported ears

These politicians march on

rallying for more laws

more violence

more death

more families separated

more borders

more code words

more media silence

What the hell kind of world are we leaving to the next generation?

one where they will have to hide their identity?

one where they will hide in the suburbs of an anonymous town and

pretend that our brothers and sisters are not being murdered in cold blood

just because no one wants to talk about it?

I have never felt welcome here

or there

I have never felt a part of anything here

or there

It has been like a giant police state since day one

whether I was being pulled over and questioned under false pretenses

or told to get the fuck out of town and never come back

by my politicians and by my educators

the lies my teacher taught me

could fill volumes

This President buries his head in the sand of the Gulf

while the blood flows into the Rio Grande

no one cared when young girls disappeared into the desert

no one cared when drug cartels slaughtered innocents

and no one cares now

if this is what you meant by hope

by change

I want no part of it

My bloodline runs through Chilili, Nuevo Mexico y Williams, Arizona

we have been here for centuries

Let us see your papers, pilgrim

Reality Show Suicide

I want high resolution stills from every single embarrassing and horrible moment in my life so that I can import them into Photoshop and manipulate them. I want digital footage of all the fucked-up things that happened - streaming audio of all the dumb shit I said.

I want my life story documented and narrated by Kurt Loder. With an introduction by Andy Rooney and with a final, closing statement read by William S. Burroughs. I want Burroughs to take his shotgun and blow apart the clay blocks that have my history written on them.

Loder would stand there next to my unconscious and puke stained body and say things like: here was a wasted youth. Here is the end result. Here is Cobain's "teen spirit" personified. Here is…

I would have these "personal moments" where I talk into the camera after doing something stupid and I would get all emotional about it. I would look into the camera and say corny shit like: You don't know me, man! This is what happens when people start getting real!

There would be dramatic music and erratic camera angles. It would be a magnificent and flaming train wreck. There would be a scene of myself sitting in the dark in a smoke-filled room with serious Phil Collins music playing in the background, philosophizing in between drags.

Of course some of the faces would be blurred to protect the innocent...but not many. There would be "witnesses" with their profiles in shadow so as not to expose them. Their voices would be digitally altered and Kurt Loder would ask them personal and intimate questions.

And there would be tears. Maybe an on-camera suicide where Kurt acts all shocked and surprised and the camera crew rushes in to help only to discover that it was all a big fucking joke with the "victim" laughing his head off. That would be me and I would do it multiple times.

Cut and paste. Add layers and masks so as to enhance the pathetic nature of so many moments in time gone awry.

But before I go
I want to vomit all of the bad moments from my life into the toilet bowl and watch them go swirling down the drain.

I want to experience everything bad all over again like so many roaches and maggots crawling all over the meat in the trash bin.

No bloodshed.
No curdled dreams on the asphalt for all to walk over and disregard.
Just the memories.

And Kurt Loder. With advertisements by all the companies that matter. In HD (where available).

Cut to commercial.

The Amerikkkan People

I tried to look up the definition of the American people

but came up with no definitive answers

I have no idea what that means: the American people

is that you?

I know it's not me

or the people they are killing on the border

shoot first ask questions later

is it my neighbor with white bootlaces and oil paintings of Hitler?

is it the kid down the block getting arrested for selling dope?

is it the house behind me with domestic abuse issues

are the collective "we" the American people? you know -

liberty and justice for some

and all of the other contrived words that

people seem to spout off about yet

rarely understand

politicians love to talk about: the American people

but they actually have no intentions of attaching those words to anyone but

those that cast dollars in their favor

there is no such thing as "the American people"

it's an idea - a euphemism for something much darker

that applies to everyone and no one simultaneously

it is the target audience of every commercial advertisement since the dawn of

mass communication

it is the all singing, all dancing crap of the nation

it is what the polls tell you it is

Clearly

clearly I'm not cut out for customer

service or sales

retail

service with a smile

or anything even remotely having to do with the

general public in any facet or form, shape, color and what have you

clearly

as I keep shooting everyone who

walks into the store in their fucking needy faces

their noses explode and eyes liquefy under heat and

pressure and blood pours out of every crater

orifice, old and new

brains spill on the tile and windows

even up into the fan, spraying my face with au du frontal lobe flambé

clearly

from the way I keep shooting the corpses, long

after they're deceased as they jump and

jerk with each new bullet hole riddled along their sickly bodies

shouting at them, shaking them

gripping their clothing tightly in my hands and pulling them

close to me

whispering into their ears: can you repeat the question?

laughing over them as the police haul me away to the dark and dank solitude

of a cell well below the earth's surface to consider what I've done clearly

below the sidewalks and sewer systems I remain,

cursing those above me and wishing them wicked outcomes

at the hands of strangers like me

on the way to my final sit down

I resemble a man torn asunder, a man pushed too far

a man who waited too long for the rain to come and wash the shit

from the streets

a man walking the final walk to the kilowatt couch, grinning

and knowing that this shall not be the end,

clearly

Hell in a Box

I want to gift wrap Hell for you

I want to put it in a little box and wrap it

with expensive colored paper and bows

I want to condense all of that evil down into a small, concise, tight package,

for you

mail it express so that you have to sign for it

I want to imagine you there, at your doorstep on a clear day

with no one else at home

bewildered by the small package before you

the one without a return address on it

I want to soak up the silence in the room

as you lurk over your little gift and wonder

who it could be from and what could be inside

I want to picture your face as you read the tiny card

that is attached to the box: surprise!

I want to hide in the shadows, silently

patiently as you tear into that neat, little package , shred by shred

pulling on the bow string and running your fingers over the smooth and

colorful paper

I want to see you remove the lid from the top of the box

I want to savor the reaction on your face

listen for the breathless scream that will not come

as you watch in terror as all of it is unleashed upon you

in your very own house and from within a tiny, colorful box with no name

I would like to be there for that…I think I shall begin to look for a box

All Things Considered

I look at your pictures and wonder

why I didn't murder you when I had the chance

it would have been relatively easy to do

all things considered

it would have landed me in the place that has been chasing me

always so elusive

but not impossible

in dreams - all of the time

smoke and welded iron

blood and cheap tile

reflective spirals of razor barbed wire

you deserved to die

you still do

but I suppose you will shuffle to your grave

a lonely and sorry excuse for a man

knowing that you sold your family

sold your friends and sold yourself

how does that feel?

there is blood on your hands

none of it your own

B Shift

When we found him he had a mouthful of gold and

frothy pink blood foaming out

almost like he had mixed some Alka-Seltzer and Pepto Bismol for fun

he hadn't done much that evening except get blasted by an anonymous shotgun

in the middle of the night

bright red blood bubbled from the holes in his lung as he gasped for air

and clutched at whatever he could grab

he wouldn't tell me who did this to him

he couldn't have been more than 15

writhing and gasping on the stretcher like some fish out of freshwater

his family members fought us all the way

screaming for answers

I watched a cop get taken down out of the corner of my eye

I wanted to be nowhere near

we loaded the kid up and closed the doors

and not long after that he was dead

Summer of 2007

They are shootin' mother fuckers here
like it's going out of style
and the people cheer!
two more added to the toll this A.M.
the summer heat has not yet begun
but the eggs are already frying on the sidewalk
amidst the White chalk outlines and under the watch of overseers
on horses, action cameras and microphones
and the almighty eye of the church downtown

This is the way the world ends
not with a bang but with bullet holes
with anonymous prayers and littered shell casings
religious pamphlets and body bags
this is where Black blood runs thick
in the streets and out to sea
as the sermons on Sunday talk tough
the pastors smile now and cry later
high as their tithing dollars will take them
this is where the colored girls go:
Doo, doo doo, doo doo, doo doo doo...
and say, hey babe
take a walk on the wild side
the bold side
the new side
same as the old side

More in Sorrow Than in Anger

and so it rains, over

its droplets opulent with the bane of

my own being

I possess no sovereignty over my volition, anymore

having long subjugated my will to

contrition

my heart coalesces, with

fear, the suffering long dealt out

without reparations, and of course

hatred

my appetite strengthens, longing

for recompense, unadulterated and unfettered

leaving me, once and again

more in sorrow than in anger, as

I recoil, along the dark colonnades

through the deep porticoes

taking shape in shadows

as Hell hath joined together

so as no man shall put asunder

this predilection of the flesh

It Keeps You Running

Everything is ridiculous

the writing has been on the wall for years now

I should know

I put it there

today I am here

wading through the bodies that float past me

one by one

like so many blow-up dolls

with their eyes open and their mouths agape

as if they cannot believe what happened

they are on their way to the end

this is the river of fuck

this is what happens after too much television

too much reality

too many Big Macs

too much porn

this is where it all gets flushed

the place no one wants to talk about

there are no billboards here

no advertising to speak of

it is quiet except for the sound of bodies floating in the water

they have been dead for years

indentured servants

plugged in

jacked up

tuned in and turned out

sitting in the family room

eyes glued to their screens

ears to their phones

oversexed and overstimulated

overfed and uneducated

ready for the climax

ready for the money shot

ready

they have all been sold down the river

by men in expensive suits

who made their fortunes on our apathy

trust and ignorance

and somewhere Billy Mays is shouting

Faux News

Get the gun oil out and start writing personal notes on your bullets

little epitaphs that say: *Fuck You!* and *Told You So, Motherfucker!*

Turn on the idiot box and watch it unfold

right before your very eyes

on the couch of your addled brains

Truth! Patriotism! The A-Merican Way!

sponsored by McDonald's, Starbucks and Wilford Brimley's Diabeetus

and brought to you by Magic Dick Pills and the Sham-Wow

This. Stuff. Really. Works.

You can see them marching from your window

their boots resounding in unison, right, left, right, left, right

they are behind the curtains pulling the strings,

screaming for freedumb - they are the shitters

the bottom dwellers

under the control of something you haven't been able to figure out

they are the all-fucking, all-dancing, shitters of the world

shitting in unison

the proverbial: *They*

Their flock has grown like so many insects hatching

out of a lying preacher's mouth

birds of a feather shit together

so lock the door and mind your Goddamned business

shut your mouth, sit still and stay tuned for these messages

because trouble is brewing

they are out there

waiting, waiting, waiting…

Shhhhhhhh!

they are insatiable and armed to the teeth

they are coming!

oh yes they are!

I can hear them at the door!

Oh fuck! They are here!

And now here's Tom with sports.

Truths & Consequences

Sometimes you run
from certain things
until you look back years later
and realize that it's only your shadow following you
step for step, line for line
mocking every move you make

Every place is exactly the same
this wasteland of vacant strip malls
over watered lawns guarding toothpick castles
and pile after pile of useless products
rotting under the sun and moon

There is no Heaven above
no Hell below
one place is as good/bad as the next
and there really wasn't anywhere to run to
in the first place

No one bothered to say anything
there is nowhere and no one
left to ask all of the questions
that have no answers
only consequences
and hard truths

It's All True

It's all true!
the President is a citizen of Kenya
an African voodoo priest with the destruction of
Main Street U.S.A. on his mind
watch out!
it was foretold by his chicken bones long ago
he is a vessel for Hitler's preserved brain
a racist who wants to put all of the White people on trains
and send them to death camps
the fourth Reich!
he is a SSSsssssssssocialist
communist, fascist, Nazi
Black devil, Black panther, Black Ops
new world order rock-and-roller
with a Black power fist raised in defiance
and he wants to kill your grandmother

9/11 was an inside job
orchestrated by a mastermind
Elvis is still alive
the moon landing was a hoax
jazz, blues and rock music are all tools of Satan
(because Satan is real and lives in the middle of the earth)
little green men kidnap hillbillies and rape them
they also turn cows inside out
Mexicans are trying to re-conquer the Southwest

Jews control everything

slavery was not that bad

Blacks are coming for your daughters and sons and

the holocaust never, ever happened

Christianity makes sense!

Jesus is a red-blooded, red state, flag-waving, card-carrying

kick-your-heathen-ass Amerikkkan!

He loves football and Natural Light

the earth is 4,000 years old and flat

the Flintstones was a documentary

the bible is to be taken literally - talking snakes and all

There is no such thing as a racist

Rush Limbaugh is drug-free

Glenn Beck is a patriot

taxes are a conspiracy

science is for faggots

reading is for commies

close the libraries

burn the books

pitchforks and powder kegs for the lizard people

it's all in the water anyway

the truth is out there

on a grassy knoll

everything is O.K.

everything is O.K.

everything is A.O.K.

It's all true

End of the Line

This is the woman in my dreams.

It's not what you think and I know what you're thinking.

Every time I jump in the red car she gives me a pensive look

and then pushes the gas pedal as far as it will go.

Each night we end up in a hail of twisted metal, fire and blood spatter

on the highway at the edge of my mind.

Each night I know better and yet I always climb inside and sit next to her.

There are no words between us, barely even a glance;

the rush of the screaming wind and trails of lights passing by

are enough to make my heart explode.

Her name is on my lips at the moment just before impact…

Jacob's Ladder

Alternate reality within a single breath

you imagine another life entirely, the witness protection program,

hiding, squatting, avoiding

living in a paradise, where you have no place,

no ticket, no refund

take a breath, close your eyes

pull the trigger, squeeze

in an instant everything clicks, only a second passes before all is lost

and you are right back where you belong

at the moment right before your death

the present has been nothing but an illusion

all along, fashioned by the mind at its finest hour

bang

All the Wrong Reasons

I pulled a gun out once

a long time ago

while we were cruising down the road in the

middle of the night and there was nothing going on

except the monotony of the radio and the boredom that

goes with not getting laid

it was a perfect moment for

all the wrong reasons

Russian roulette at the stop light

these kids, yelling and gesturing from their expensive car

in their expensive clothes and shiny class rings

wanting to get it on and draw some blood

gritting their teeth and spitting mere words

not really knowing how close they are to the edge

I will never forget watching their faces

as we waited for the light to turn green

time dripping by

as I laid the shotgun barrel along the open window frame

in the backseat of the car

pointed at their smug faces

cocking my head to the side

ever so slowly as the smallest of all grins

creases my face

and in that moment, all of the bullshit

all the ridiculousness of a suburban teenage existence

all of the endless and boring summer nights

all of the what if's and the missed opportunities

to be something, be someone

to do anything original

all went out the window

I relished their fear right then

the blood draining from their faces

the smell of freshly burned tires on asphalt

the silence afterward

they will never know if the gun was loaded at all

or even real

and the light did eventually turn green

No Justice, Just Us

Uniformed police officers

that is, the overseers of the so-called peace

the enforcers of the so-called law

patrolling these United States of Plantations

serving, protecting and sometimes murdering

leaving in their wake

death and taxes

upon those who either see them as savior

or merely slaver

They are sworn in and armed accordingly

dressed in creased and pressed suits that hold

     all of the traits

     all of the flaws

     all of the symptoms

     all of the weaknesses

     all of the ugly and dark shit

that only we know about deep, down inside

where prejudice prevails over the common good

They have all of these things and more

just like the rest of us -

me, you and officer Johannes Mehserle

who is sitting in his protective custody prison cell

at this very moment

a broker of power over marginalized communities of color

wearing yet another uniform, bloodstained

he is unmoved, unchanged and unchained

no different from the days of whips and horsebacks

These uniforms do not magically absolve anyone from fault

but the guilt that sometimes flows from the seams and stitches

washes away freely as if somehow wearing the uniform itself

is penance enough

    if a killer dons a shiny badge

    if a bigot drapes a robe

    if a sadist takes an oath

they all end up gifted with knee-jerk authority

lawyer-proof credibility and the unwavering respect of the general public

along with a 'get out of jail free card'

just in case they happen to murder someone in cold blood

without any other excuse except for a shrug

and maybe a quiet apology

because they know

    there is no justice

    there is just us

The People You Murder In Your Sleep

There is no beginning and no ending

only what I remember and even that is in more pieces

than all the parts of my scrambled mind

combined

laundry rooms I have never set foot in

bodies hanging from hooks in the ceiling

neon lights and passing traffic on streets I used to know

details always escape me come morning

and nothing is ever the same

twice

I know that I revisit past events

sometimes differently than how they originally occurred

what purpose does dreaming about murder serve

am I merely killing an idea…?

I wake up with memories of unlocking various minds

some with baseball bats and others with scalpels

peering inside with an immeasurable rage

I watch myself perform the act

there is never any fatigue and no one says: cut!

it goes on and on with a sound much like

a home run in the middle of an empty field

I see people that I used to know in another life

I remember what they used to be like and

compare that with what I have heard about them

through so-called social media

some of them have taken their own lives

others have betrayed themselves

others no longer speak at all

others still only keep up appearances

while secretly wishing for death

but they all appear in dreams

and I wake up every morning with blood on my hands

We Do Nothing

they tell us they are going to kill us and we do nothing

they tell us they are going to rob us and we do nothing

they tell us they are feeding us poison and we do nothing

they say they are going to rape us and we do nothing

they say they are lying to us and we do nothing

we.do.nothing.

they say: we will sacrifice your sons and daughters for profit

they say: this is the new slavery

they say: we will scorch the earth

they say: there will be nothing left

they say: we will erase your memories

they say: we will brainwash your children's children

they say:

no food

no rights

no jobs

no money

no health

no happiness

no opinions

no life

we.do.nothing.

we sit comfortably in our warm suburban homes
in our gated communities
cut off from anything even remotely real
we pipe in all of this information through
cables and wires and invisible satellite beams
we chew the fat and digest it and
wrinkle our noses at the idea
of anything
anywhere
any time

we.do.nothing.

we are so many corpses with empty sockets and
empty pockets sitting around the family television
with shit-eating grins
absorbing the constant stream of lies like
rays of sunshine
from the church of the digital
while fires roar in the background
burning up any remaining books filled with knowledge
as we do nothing because

we.are.nothing.

Lifetime

Sometimes I think I should still be there

I have always had this feeling of being on borrowed time

I am haunted by it

Like breaking into the gates of paradise only to be arrested

sometime later and hauled back down to Hell by cops with an agenda

everything I have experienced flushed down the drain

it causes me to look nervously into the rear-view mirror

watching for death

listening for him to say: time's up, mother fucker!

maybe I should still be there,

experiencing 10 years of overdue mediocrity

taking what's due in good stride

the interest on my penance must be something

I should be there

standing in the street with no excuses

waiting for something to happen

with nothing but the wind from the sky and the dirt from the street

to blow past me

and sometimes I do see myself there

waiting to die

standing there as a car comes furiously down the lonely road

I see its bright headlights upon me

it's not until after it sends me flying through the air

that I realize that everyone I have ever wronged is in the car

they have all been waiting

some of them for a lifetime

Ravenous

I want to eat your mind, whole and raw

on delicate white porcelain with

sharp, murderous-looking utensils

your thoughts, your secrets, your private innuendos

I want them

I want to slice into the library of your consciousness,

take a book off of the shelf and ingest it whole

maybe your pineal gland to begin

chew into your medulla oblongata

page by page

gnash your brain stem with my pearly whites,

for just a moment

chew, relish, swallow, repeat

bit by meaty bit, savoring each morsel

drinking your juices and inhaling the aroma

that is so uniquely you

as I swallow your thoughts down into my pit

waiting for my own mechanisms

to break them down even further

and spit them out again

Riverdale

I never thought I would live in Riverdale

But here I am

The whole gang is here

Archie's head

is no longer attached to his body

it's in a plastic bag in the freezer

probably freezer-burned by now

Veronica and Betty are tied up in the back

but they won't be alive for long

and when Jughead starts his car today it will explode

incinerating his body and leaving only the charred remains of that stupid hat

I dumped the body of Mrs. Grundy in his trunk as well

I wonder if any of it will survive

Will they blame Jughead for her murder?

Reggie is sliced up and separated into 20 trash bags

and ready for disposal into the river

there are others on the list

I am going one by one

I never intended to live here

But here I am

Car Wrecks Sent From Heaven and Other Hilarious Jokes to Tell Grieving Parents

god does not work in mysterious ways

god does not send pick-up trucks careening into ice cream parlors

to collect the souls of three-year-olds

because he missed them

god does not leave misery in the aftermath

of suicides and misgivings

or meddle in the stupid or the fucking mundane

(s)he does not

we do all that by ourselves

there is no god of misery

things like that happen because we make them so

that is, after all, the most horrific part of being alive

there is the moment just before death

when you realize

you were wrong

that last look, gasp, clench;

the final realization

like God's laughing reflection on the water

joke's on us

always has been

laugh it up

End of the Line 2

She is always in the driver's seat

she shows up in dreams

no words, ever

she forever has that smirk upon her face

which isn't really a smile and so I'm never sure if she's annoyed or amused

we are lovers

no…we are adversaries

No

we are and we are not

it's never the same

it's her eyes that speak the most language

and tell me whether I am on my way to my death

or just another road trip down memory lane

I never know until the moment before consciousness

and like that, she is gone again and I am awake

no wiser than when my eyes closed and still without her name

Gun Powder, Psalms & Shrapnel

Everyone is ready to
die
As ready as the first
Natives
watching the pilgrims come
ashore
arms outstretched and gifts in
wait

#

I walked up the twelve steps
and saw how pathetic the rest of them looked
what a bunch of assholes! Not me, man...
it made me so sick that I threw myself back down the stairs
on the way back down I heard them calling after me with words of
encouragement and spiritual enlightenment
I realized that I should set fire to the staircase and start digging
yes, dig deep they said
it's going to be a long way down
I'll let you know when I get there

I have a drawer full of bullets

I found most of them on the street

at crime scenes

while taking dead people

to the dying place

in my spare time I paint names on them

with the care and precision

of a surgeon

one of these days I'm going to give the bullets

to their rightful owners

here's yours

\#

Another beautiful

Jacksonville day

bullet-ridden corpses

with a chance

of afternoon showers

fear, loathing

and lots of unanswered prayers

Bottle of Jack

check

small bag of weed

check

pack of smokes

check

super cheap hooker

check

two bullets

one for her

one for me

Bang

#

I dreamed you

in satin and lace

veiled behind a thin curtain

blood red paint upon your lips

your lithe figure

in moonlight spilling along the backdrop

you were waiting for me

a single razor blade behind your back

glinting in the light

waiting to slice into my flesh

I feel like I'm in the witness protection program

when I am not doped up on fast food, alcohol or reality TV

when I am not jacked in to the matrix

I realize that I am on borrowed time

that any moment the feds could kick the door down and haul my ass to prison

for a lifetime of being Mr. Fuck-up;

can you see the real me?

no, you cannot

no one can because I have run away and changed my name

I am a stranger in a strange land

living the life on borrowed time with an assumed name

#

Buzzards in the desert sky

swooping down to inspect the flesh, fresh

half-rare from time spent under the sun

left out among lies, trash and thievery of scavengers past

rusted-out cars line the roadmarkers for the dead

memories that left them there

so much waste and decay these days and evermore

dead skeleton hands

sticking up from the sands

reveal secrets from long ago and

scars thought long outgrown

I ought to drill holes in myself
carve dark craters deep into my flesh
let all the poison pour out and spill down into the dirt
making the earth below my feet turn a darker shade as
what dwells within leaks down and seeps in, bubbling
there's too much bad material floating around inside of me
things you wouldn't want to think about
stuff better left unspoken
my innards bathed with false hopes
yearnings and earnings waged from
bitter times
maybe I should pour it all into mason jars
then sell them one by one to deviants and tyrants
rich men looking to buy the one thing that doesn't have a price

\#

peddle the flesh
sell your soul on eBay
highest bidder gets to shoot you in the face
sign around your neck
says: I believe
cut you into little pieces
sear on one side
serve with watermelon consumé
garnish with hopes and dreams
bon appétit

I am like garbage today

a walking landfill of excess,

complete with trash-birds eating pieces

as they please and the rats crawling in and out

I am hung over and swollen

I am caked in the blood of liars

mannequins everywhere and

not enough chainsaws

this is the mall of Amerikkka

strip mall wasteland

I want to stick a grenade in your mouth

pull the pin

watch the fireworks

boom!

\#

Ocean water washes in red tide day by day

bringing sand littered with pieces of different civilizations

strewn across the landscape like the remains of

a bazaar torn apart by fire

we walk among these pieces barefoot

a canvas streaked with unnatural colors

and trinkets from a bygone era

the tide rolls out again

and we walk away

pretending not to look

occasionally stopping to take a piece for a souvenir

A dinner in hell

amidst the burning sinners

sipping sour wine out of broken glasses

serenaded by their screams

and fallen angels

the sky is falling indeed

it is the way of all flesh

#

You are a rotten [apple]

    your [core] is corrupt

poison [seeds]

    maggots and [worms[

strewn throughout [stem] to pit

#

As ashes to water

fire storms to earth

I appease the one within

the shadow

hidden tightly inside

peeking from behind ordinary eyes

sociopath isn't politically

correct any longer

these days, we say:

antisocial behavior disease

highly treatable

with little pills and then

talk about your feelings

or lack thereof

wait for results

like baking a cake

Jeff and Ted missed out

#

Jailhouse preacher sings

save your soul

save your soul

save your soul for Gee-suhz!

but there is never enough penance to pay the bill

so we are subjected to debt collectors

pay up mother fucker

I see you in the photograph with frayed edges
there's a date written on the back
you are an old ghost with dead eyes
the carnival door that leads to your heart
no longer entices because
I buried you long ago and now I'm afraid to look back
and see you digging yourself out of the ground
your hand busting up through the earth and clawing after me
you can leave all the messages you want, written in lipstick
on my bathroom mirror
I won't be calling again

\#

my thoughts drift to dreams never had
I can't help but think of how I'd like to carve
a small piece of your flesh
from the bone and cook it in a dull spoon
over a candle flame until it liquefies
I'd then draw up your essence into a syringe
and shoot you into my bloodstream;
pure, unadulterated and clean
the ultimate high

You are dead to me
I watch the veins in my hand run dark
as I read your words
your musings, stale and spiteful
I inhale your emotions like smoke
and blow them back in your face
flick the cigarette, cherry red
at your chest, watch the ashes fly
and tell you to fuck off
this last bullet is for myself
I wrote my name on it years ago
I guess it's finally time:
stupid o'clock
words like hate
rivulets of the stuff,
green like poison
traveling my veins and circulating through my heart
if I spit at you
it would burn like acid

I'm sitting in the dark

smoking cigarettes and filling the room with stale and heavy smoke

the radio is on in the background

it's Art Bell

he's talking to men making death threats

I want to call the show but

I suspect I would not have the courage to say anything

because I know that they are out there, listening

there's just silence in the background as I clutch the cord and listen

Art says: Hello? Caller are you there…?

And then click

someone is knocking at the door

\#

If I thought it would help

I would go out on the streets and

kill the ones that deserve it

but I know now that their numbers are too great

and it would not make any difference

the evil that men do goes on and on

while the news just reports mundane and idiotic shit

they live

and I have lost my sunglasses

I cannot sleep

I do not

my mind wanders endlessly

revisiting vast cemeteries on the edge of nothingness

huge graveyards at the ends of cliffs

surrounded by fog and rotten animals that hunger for flesh

my mind drifts there

unearthing ghosts of war

I replay full-scale battles

inside of my own private theater

#

When we are children it is easy to ask the difficult questions

there is always someone there to answer them

even if they do not always know

they lie

it is comforting to have someone wise

this fades over time

you are left

with your reflection and the tiny voice inside of your head

some questions do not have answers

some questions beg not to be asked

your voice alone has the only answers that suffice

and sometimes those are not good enough

this is how we take tiny steps closer to death

in the dark

and without answers

wrath is the most bitter addiction

the words of a witch from the [past]

still echo in my heart about

my insatiable lust for agreement

and my codependent relationship with rage

flip the switch

flip the switch

flip it

ain't nothing changed but my blood pressure and reflexes

\#

I am broken

a bad m a c h i n e

walking the wrong way

around the wheel

a reject from the factory

with an inheritance of manufactured sin

I know that the factory is automated and cold

I know myself

I know that God is dead

I know

because I am from the factory

I make the machines

I am the reverend with no congregation

preaching to a flock that has long since lost their faith

wandering in the valley of the shadow

on a mule too forlorn for want of drink

there are nothing but bleached bones in the sand

wrought with marks from scavengers

The wind talks to me, carrying the confessions of ghosts, they whisper:

there is no god, preacherrr...no salvation

only thisss death

join ussss

and so I do

#

As the blade crosses your delicate

throat

the blood spills out and lands on the black lacquer

surface

like millions of tiny red diamonds

each unique and

shimmering

I punch the dead man but he does not react

I don't know what I expect as

he swings back and forth in the cold air

I punch him again and once more

nothing - just the same stupid look on his face

the sound of the hooks in his flesh, creaking

the dead do not fight back

instead they only stare back at you with their comeuppance

that all knowing glare that says:

hit me all you want, you stupid fuck

I'm dead

#

you're already rotting

and I wonder where you are

eaten alive?

merely decomposing?

or are you some place more ominous

someplace dark,

biding your time

and planning evil things?

hard to say

devil in a white suit

maybe one day I'll find out

I saw her that day

just a little girl with a bullet hole in her head

I saw her lifeless and bloody body pulled

out of the back of the rescue unit in the ambulance bay

I saw the look of fear on men who are not supposed to have fear

I will never forget her

#

Wanting

to

dip my head

in a bath of acid

in hopes

that memories

of you will be

eaten away

#

If we allow people to die in the street

empty their bank accounts to pay

Wallstreet bonuses

if we produce nothing

consume everything

allow our children to languish and idolize perpetual losers

what kind of people are we?

I am Wayne Gale

life is played by Mickey Knox and I

am biding my time and pretending not to be intimidated by a sociopathic

killer during our interview

there's an ending but it's a surprise

every one dies in the end

#

The past ain't nothin' but an old song

playing on the jukebox

in some rundown little hole in the wall

on a street who's name I can't remember

just on this side of nowhere

I will sometimes stumble in for a drink and

sit at the bar while the music wafts into my brain

triggering memories that are better than the originals

one hit wonders and

songs best left unheard

Sometimes you run from certain things
until you look back and realize that your shadow
follows you everywhere
everyplace is the same
this wasteland of vacant strip malls
and over-watered lawns
one place is as good or bad as the next
and there really wasn't anywhere to run to
in the first place

#

I stick the needle in you
because that's what I am supposed to do
not because you need it
not because it's the right thing to do
not because you are asking me to help you
but because it is a reaction to a situation that I have been trained for
my sympathy has long since departed
I feel nothing for you
I do not even know you
You are less than nothing to me, a body
to practice on until the next life and death situation comes along

Nothing makes much sense anymore
logic, it seems, is for assholes and bookworms
and who the fuck wants to be educated in this slave new world…?
the writing is on the TV
keep them dumb
they say
burn the books
they say
baptize them in the waters of new media religion and rhetoric
misinformation masturbation
because,
once they own all of the eyes and ears
it will not matter how many mouths are talking all at once
we really are
the all dancing, all tweeting, crap of the world
we can march into another country and murder a so-called evil man
because it's profitable
never because he is evil
because if that was the reason there wouldn't be anyone left to kill
and we would all live in one big Amerikkka
but they don't teach that kind of shit in the history books anymore
freedom.
freedom...
freedom!
we now return you to your regularly scheduled program
with no further commercial interruptions

I'm going to douse myself in gasoline and then drink cheap lighter fluid
I'm going to light a candle in the other room and wait for the fumes to travel
I'm going to inhale death, wholesale
breathe out fire and belch embers from deep down in the core
I'm going to clean my pipes out
light up the furnace
put more coal on the fire

I want to burn it all down
I want to burn from the inside out and feel everything inside of me melting
All of it
I want to burn hot
I want to ignite like a straw man in the middle of a desert
I want to vomit sparks and smoldered pieces of ash

I want to feel the pain searing through and cleaning everything out
flames funneling along every vessel, bone to nerve
my skin will shrink, tighten and dissolve exposing and singeing every muscle
tendon and piece of sinew that remains, leaving nothing unscathed
the melted fat will drip down and boil
leaving only charred bone behind
I want to burn.

The greatest fear of all

is not death itself

but instead playing with matches

one too many times

burning down the only meaningful relationships

I have left

like some withered forest

begging to be torched

and dying alone

Amerikkkan Stories

All Hookers Are Not Created Equal

There is nothing quite as satisfying as eating a bag full of greasy fast-food in a parking lot amidst the ambiance of a city run amok by blood lust and bloated news headlines. Welcome to Jacksonville, Florida – where the murder rate, the drug dealers, the hookers and the homeless make the fatty food taste all that much more succulent somehow during an otherwise uneventful lunch hour.

The scene: a semi-empty strip mall parking lot located somewhere off of Interstate 95 in the northeastern part of the sunshine state. I sat there in a fully air-conditioned ambulance with my boots unzipped, listening to The Eagles' "Life in the Fast Lane" quietly hum in the background as I ate my food and stared at the bus stop not more than twenty feet in front of me. My partner, completely oblivious to my observations, slept peacefully on the stretcher in the back of the bus.

Now when I say that I was staring at the bus stop what I actually mean is that I was staring at the people there waiting for the bus, in particular an attractive woman sitting there on the wood and concrete bench with the 1-800-ASK-DAVE ad on it. Unbeknownst to many, I know quite a bit about public transportation and the kind of people that utilize it. Not only was I exposed to the wonders of public transportation (it's cheap!) at a very young age but I was again exposed (ok, forced is a better word due to a blown car engine, drug habit and lint-filled pockets) to its charms as a young but delusional man.

The people that ride the bus are like an all-star cast of vaudeville performers that are identical in just about every burg from here to there and every little shithole in between. Sure the lines may change some and the backdrops are slightly more appealing in some cities but the characters remain the same.

There are, of course, the ordinary people that have no choice but to ride their city's public transportation for whatever reason, be it poverty, bad luck, etc. These seemingly ordinary characters do not make any waves, eye contact or pay much attention to the carnival that is public transportation around them. They simply blend in and try not to get noticed…or stabbed. They are but minor characters.

One of the more popular players is the homeless guy, which, depending on the stature of your particular burg, can be one guy or many guys. They can be crazy or quiet, funny or scary – naked or clothed. However they will always be malodorous and constant. The bus to them is a makeshift shelter on wheels where no one dare tell them otherwise, least of all the bus driver. The homeless ride and ride and ride until they are removed by the police, are beat up by thugs or until they spot something more enticing than cushy, crusted bus seats to nap on; say a dumpster full of fresh, thrown-away food from your favorite greasy spoon.

There are numerous other characters in this play including but not limited to; the gangster (both the wannabe variety and the bona fide, real

McCoy tough guy) , the hustler (whom I have had personal experience losing money to), the pervert, the puking drug addict, the crazy old lady who shouts obscenities, the loud old guy who knows you, the screaming children who will not sit down and the parent who ignores them, the guy smoking weed on the bus, the obvious (to you) serial killer, the really unconvincing and hairy transsexual, the talkative foreigner who doesn't speak English, the pimp, and lastly (and the point of this story) the hooker.

Modern day hookers may or may not look like actual hookers. This has been proven time and again by numerous documentaries on HBO. Much of how they present themselves depends on where you live and how lax the local prostitution laws are. I, myself, am no stranger to the observation of prostitutes; in fact I would say that at one time, observing the behavior and mating habits of modern day prostitutes was almost a hobby during the boring and not so boring hours at work. While scouring the streets behind the wheel of an ambulance in search of anything even remotely interesting in order to kill time, you eventually find things that do. One of them is waving money at hookers.

Unless it is blatantly obvious (like New York City obvious) it is often difficult to discern whether a person is a hooker or not. What exactly are the qualifiers you may ask? Well, in this day and age, just because a female is dressed provocatively – that does not exactly qualify her as a member of the sex industry working force. If you do not believe me I encourage you to visit your local mall and do some people watching.

In fact, so many women dress the part these days that if H.G. Wells' "Time Traveller" were to fast-forward to our present time, he may think that we have evolved into a species of pimps and ho's instead of Morlocks and Eloi and he may not be all that far off. For not all hookers are created equal and certainly they do not all look alike.

All of this observation begs the question: if a scantily clad woman sits nervously at the bus stop looking at each passing car for some kind of connection does that raise a red flag? Does it matter if she does not seem to want to get on any of the buses? How about the fact that she walks away from the bus stop only to walk back to it again and repeat the whole process? Honestly, I have no idea if it means a damn thing but it makes you wonder while digesting the finer things fast food has to offer your stomach.

So I speculated – losing a few French fries to the nether region of the space underneath my seat – I thought for a second that the game was so obvious that just maybe the bus stop prostitute was not a prostitute at all but instead, bait. Bait! Bait designed to lure in guys who might not be so contented with their fries or orange sodas. Guys who would end up with their mugs printed in some weekly advocate rag for all to see and mock; guys who do the hanky panky and pay cold, hard cash for the privilege.

I had seen such things before of course; once, while administering CPR to a crackhead next to a dumpster behind the naval recruitment center on Philips Highway, I was witness to a prostitution sting the likes of which you would see on COPS, minus the reggae beat. Other than the truckloads of dumbasses being booked I noticed one glaring detail; the "prostitutes" were all attractive.

These women were unlike the toothless whores I usually carted off to the emergency room for "severe lower back pain" and a "prolapsed uterus". These were not your usual, run of the mill, I-could-be-the-living-dead hookers. They were, in fact, female police officers dolled-up to look the part and I am sure they all hated their job. The whole ordeal made me realize that, like so many other things in life, if it looks too good to be true it probably is.

Mulling this over while getting down to the latter half of my orange soda and nary a bite or two left of my triple burger with cheese, I decided that the bus stop hooker was, in all likelihood, a cop. I also figured that I might be on camera stuffing my face and staring like a lunatic at a female cop dressed up like a hooker.

Part of me wanted to just go over and ask her but I decided that was out of the question because a) if she was a cop I'd probably get busted for soliciting and b) if she wasn't a cop I might get propositioned by a hooker and the last time that happened it turned out to be a guy in a dress. It would have to remain one of those unknowns.

Settled in the fact that I would never know the truth I crumpled my fast food bag and shifted the vehicle into reverse, wholly intent on taking just one last look. The woman, who was still sitting at the bus stop and now waving to cars and smiling, looked back at me for a moment as if almost to say: are you interested or looking to arrest me?

As I exited the parking lot a call came up on the radio. I hit the lights and siren only to merge back onto the highway, no wiser than when I arrived and in search of real hookers, who, unlike the woman at the bus stop, would tell me just about anything to get a ride to the emergency room for free drugs.

Hit And Run

I hit Donny with my car once. It was on purpose. He didn't die or anything but that was the extent of our friendship: him lying on the ground bleeding and me driving away. That and the fact that we both dated the same manipulative girl at one point or another. But I did hit him.

Was I drunk? I honestly don't remember – not that it would have been out of the ordinary for myself at that time. I did it with a midnight blue 1983 Chrysler Fifth Avenue. He denies it ever happened but I know better and so does that car if it's still around. But before I sent Donny's body flying into the asphalt on Tennyson Street he and I had never formally met. So it came as a complete shock, right before I hit him, when he tried to urinate on the side of my vehicle. I suppose I should back up a little…

Donny and I used to work together at a shitty amusement park. He worked in the games section while I worked over in food service. He was a wiry little prick with bad acne who lived with his older brother. He thought he was very funny and a lady's man but I knew better. He and I dated the same girl who somehow had us both fooled into thinking she was not a manipulative, drug-dealing, carpet-munching, hairy bitch. So we had that much in common.

The first time I saw a chick take large and colorful anal beads up her ass was at Donny's house. We all walked in and saw that he had a porno tape playing on the television. The volume was up real loud and he was fascinated by the images on the screen, which were recorded in great detail.

To be perfectly honest we were all fascinated by the movie. It was as horrific as it was exhilarating to watch; much like the mythical "donkey show" I imagine. Before then, none of us knew such things were possible…well, none of us except for Donny. He had an entire collection of flicks like that one.

When I hit Donny with my car it was after a party during the summer of 1991. We were on the very edge of Denver's once notorious "north side" neighborhood and things got a little out of hand. My friend, whom I will refer to as the Fat Man, had been sucker punched in the mouth and wanted to leave the party, which wasn't a problem because our other friend Fish was waiting for us at the not-so-world-famous Triple B pool hall. Fish was a member of the Bloods except that he drove a blue car but that's a another story entirely.

Drunk-ass Donny staggered out of the garage and over to the side of my car and said that he was going to take a piss all over it. I calmly explained to Donny that if he pissed on my car I was going to hit him with it. Sure enough he zipped down his pants and I put the car in drive and mowed him down.

Like a deer in headlights, he crumpled up on the asphalt like some asshole clutching his hip and screaming for help. I drove up next to him and rolled my window down, which only made the wailing louder so I sped off and went to go play pool with Fish and the Fat Man. Nothing happened after that because Donny was too drunk to remember what happened. No cops came and no one much talked about it because the only witnesses were myself, Fat Man and Donny.

Not many people remember Donny anymore. He was the first person I ever hit with a motorized vehicle. He's a bartender now at one of those mega-fun places where they combine everything that sucks about America and charge you for it. It's of absolutely no consequence now. Chances are you will never meet Donny but he's still around. He still owes people money and he still talks a lot of shit. And he's still just as ugly and unfunny as when we first met. For him, that summer will never end. For myself there are far too many fuck-ups to forget.

Getting Gonzo Wrong: The Cult of Hunter S. Thompson

Hunter S. Thompson had a profound influence on me as a person and as a writer. His style of writing and his antihero lifestyle had much to do with my own experimentation with drugs and alcohol as well as my bitter foray into journalism and writing in general. I know Thompson's work quite well as I have spent over half of my life studying it. When he died I was disappointed but not at all surprised; he did in fact predict his own suicide. That's not something most people put into print. Thompson was as unique as they come.

The cult of Hunter S. Thompson lives on and yet it is rather disappointing to watch his legacy fall to the side as mere pop culture and t-shirt fodder. I do not believe many people understand what Hunter S. Thompson was really about and those that do are a dying breed. The man has become an American icon; every bit as commonplace as Andy Warhol's tomato can and colored Monroe. Yet Thompson is a mere caricature of his former self and not by his own hand. His followers have done this to him through years of distorted imagery and outright embellishment of what was a career of excess and debauchery laced with serious political opinions and intense loathing of a system gone awry.

Thompson had a unique gift for words, one that was tied more to his worldview than his command of the English language, but few people idolize him as a writer. Instead they worship him as a prophet of anarchy and narcotics; a guru of the inebriated arts and Zen master of being anti-establishment. Thompson was extremely patriotic; he took drugs and alcohol as an escape from reality and he nursed a love/hate relationship with the very politics that he became famous for writing about.

In the end he was a slave and a stranger to a system that, over time, disgusted him. The reality of what modern politics turned into revolted him as much as the death of print. Popular culture has taken his likeness and put it on t-shirts, coffee mugs and bumper stickers. They emulate the caricature, not the man – but I suppose we do this to all of our antiheroes in one form or another. They become more mythic than anything and we carry that flame (sometimes blindly) because it is all we have to cling to.

Thompson chased the American dream and ended up with an army of followers misinterpreting his legacy. What a prize it must be to become king of a nation that you cannot relate to. He killed himself for a reason; one which he chose years before his death and at the heart of which is the decline of western civilization. Gonzo journalism is not only widely misunderstood but also a dead art form. I am not sure it was ever truly understood to begin with.

There's a whole generation of pill-poppers out there with low-top deck shoes and cigarette holders in their mouths, wearing the reflection of a decaying civilization in their dark aviator's shades and reciting gonzo quotes without understanding what they mean. The world did not get old, Hunter Thompson did. Politics never change, people do. That is difficult to understand for the ones that idolize him as a classic hero wielding the pen over the sword.

People see Thompson's indulgence in drugs and anarchy as something to celebrate and they view his wild and chaotic paragraphs and Ralph Steadman's portrayals of him as gospel. It all paints a picture of a man in search of the American dream; a man crazed on acid and ether and too many broken typewriter keys. But therein lies the irony – Thompson did not cover shitty events (or even good ones) with the aid of a BlackBerry or a laptop. He was old school – all the way to the bitter end. The proverbial "they" have detailed his descent into altered consciousness with so much romance and bravado that the original text hardly compares to the mythology anymore and no one can imagine doing what he did with simple pen and paper much less an outdated tape recorder or typewriter.

Almost the entire cult of Hunter S. Thompson revolves around a single short story, loosely based in factual events. Truth be told, a single movie portrayal of that story has more to do with the perception of the man than anything he ever actually wrote. But Thompson is more than one story, one film or one single word. In fact he has a whole body of work, spanning decades, most of which people fail to seek out. Thompson did not start out working at Rolling Stone, nor did he gain a nation of followers overnight. He clawed his way there through years of sheer and utter misery covering stories that would cause most modern readers to chuck whatever rag it was printed on into the trash, author be damned.

No one but another journalist can understand Hunter's passion. Most journalists however, do not go around quoting Hunter S. Thompson or inhaling ether – they are too busy cursing themselves for choosing journalism as a profession in the first place. You can have all of the idealistic fuck-arounds to Las Vegas that you want, complete with a trunk full of drugs, booze and dreams but nothing will get you to the high water mark of Hunter's loathing like covering small-town news, local politics and taking pictures of the local brats as they massacre Horatio Algier on stage.

Journalism, true gritty, chain-smoking, tiny liquor bottle journalism is dead. It died with Thompson a long time ago. It has been dead for quite some time with many an editor trying to shock it back to life with outdated equipment and out-of-touch talent. Thompson knew this. What we have today is mass misinformation-sharing at the speed of light and beyond.

We ingest everything instantaneously and worry about its meaning later…or never. Nothing means anything anymore and the time that it did mean something was short. Thompson single-handedly documented a generation – he would be vastly irrelevant were he starting out today – not because he wouldn't be brilliant but because there are scant few listening.

Print is dead. No one even bothers to read the writing on the wall and there is a massive amount of it that goes ignored. There are still suckers wishing they would have never mentioned the word "journalism" sitting in some dismal elementary auditorium, taking notes on the first act of Othello as portrayed by the local Eighth grade class – waiting there and hoping the building catches fire so there will be something decent to pad into their technology. But those people are not Hunter's legacy nor do they claim to channel the man's spirit.

Journalists are a breed unlike any other. It's cutthroat and dire; the only reward at the end of the road is a bullet in the head and thousands of littered memoirs where real dreams go to die. Thompson knew this. He documented it and his words live on, even if they are misunderstood.

McRape

I do not want my children to establish meaningful relationships with corporate mascots. If they do, I will not be responsible for it. I do not want that blood on my hands. I do not wish to treat them like little drug addicts that need their next fix from a pimp in clown makeup.

I think it's disgusting that children identify with corporations at all. From the cradle to the grave is what they want in a customer. We should all be ashamed of ourselves for letting it go this far…but I know that we are not. I believe we are selling our children into a kind of slavery that we will never break free from ourselves – but we at least had a choice. Our own slavery is one that we entered into willingly. We all shook hands with the Devil and let him slake our thirst for convenience and give unto us the gift of unending desire for sugar, fat and salt.

If there is a Devil he looks like Ronald McDonald. He comes bearing gifts and he wants all of our children. He will eat their hearts and collect their heads like so many trophies on the wall; miles and miles of tiny heads, each one happier than the last. He sits atop a mountain of little heads; his mouth blood-stained and with a perma-smile upon his face – his kingdom for our children.

That's brand loyalty.

He's your momma, he's your daddy, he's that nigga in the alley, he's your doctor when in need (want some Coke, have some fries), you know him, he's your friend, your main boy, thick and thin, he's your pusherman.

You invite him into your home, sit him at the dinner table and smile as he shoves a needle into your lusting veins. He hangs his IV bag and laughs as you fade into a corn-fed and syrup coma. I'd call it "rape" but you invited him over after all, as well as paid for the privilege of his company.

Ronald will fuck you and take your children with him to collect their hearts and heads. He will leave you strung out and hollow and he will always be back for more. He will eat your soul from the inside out and come 'round late at night to make sure you fulfill your part of the bargain.

If it's any consolation, you are not alone. He has raped billions. He is in fact the greatest serial rapist the United States of Corporations has ever known. He will fuck you and make a commercial out of it. You will smile and play to the camera. They will call it McRape.

You're lovin' it.

Snake Eyes

All of the false and made-up reasons that the United States of Amerikkka went to war so many years ago are resolved. Just look around. The only enemies left are the ones the State has falsely convinced us to accuse: our own neighbors. Saddam Hussein is long dead. Longtime US ally and now allegedly deceased boogieman, Osama Bin Laden is dead.

The "bad guys" are all dead and we royally fucked all of their supporters up the ass to the umpteenth power- millions of them. We have flags in all of our enemies territories. We have stolen natural resources coming out of our own asses and were this a game of Risk, the box would have been put away a long time ago.

But it's not a game of Risk, instead it's Monopoly. It's always been Monopoly. That's our foreign policy, all under the guise of "freedom", "democracy" and "fair play". It's all bullshit.

All of this on the day that the feel-good President of the decade quietly extends the most revolting legislation of our time. Captain Marketing himself, all smiles and little substance, signed on the dotted line, thus extending much of what abhorred everyone the last time around.

Tell a good joke or two, go get the bad guy and slam dunk it in everyone's slack-jawed faces - that's marketing Billy Graham style. Hope? Change?

Blah.

Do not pass Go and report directly to jail - this mother fucker is putting up hotels and we all just rolled snake eyes.

Everlasting Night

The night stretches into day with the sun and moon blurred by the streetlights and cold stares of passersby. I do not sleep any longer. I cannot. I drift in and out of people's nightmares, sometimes as a spectator and others as an active participant. They never know my name and I rarely bother to mention it. It's not important.

I spill blood on the floor only to clean it up in an endless ritual that serves to benefit no one. I wander the same hallways and look at the same portraits on the walls – the same stale corporate art. I walk past the same grieving rooms every night and hear different families sobbing over the same death.

I see them all lying there beyond the walls and doors, beyond plain sight, waiting to be catered to and carried away. Everyone that bursts through the doors is on their own planet. Some of them I recognize and others I do not. We are all the same and we are all different. We are all on the same collision course and we all dance with death.

I'm fat now, washed up, doped and glassy-eyed from an overdose of fast food and too many Cokes and coffee. Despite the fact I have easy access to narcotics and sedatives it seems the only thing that will do is a hit of the most powerful drug: sleep, but I have long given up on that elusive whore.

I am confused and beaten down. I feel greasy and unfettered. I deal with liars and monsters and the living dead. There is of course the occasional "patient" but they are too few and far between to matter. There are far too many needful parasites that crave attention like a drug and they all seem to crave it in the middle of the night.

I can see them for what they are underneath the surface of their skin. They only want me for what I can give them and for where I can take them. It's like a slow-motion revolving door. When all the giving is done they depart back into the night and I forget them just as quickly as I discovered them.

The emergency room is bathed in a sanitized fluorescent light that reflects off of the blood puddles on the tile below. There is a cacophony of curse words and medical jargon; prayers and last rites. Death hides behind every curtain with a dagger in one hand and a consolation prize in the other.

Though I've walked through this place a thousand times it always manages to look just a little different. There are always new faces with the same old stories to tell. I watch as the double doors swing open and two large policemen haul a broken and bloody pulp of a man into the room. He is shirtless and still has barbs and small wires sticking out of his chest, fresh from who knows how many jolts of electricity.

The two men slam him down into a chair and handcuff him to a rail on the wall. "This one's just begging for more," one of them says. They high five each other and walk out the doors again. I can hear their laughter and footsteps fade just as the sound of a helicopter from above drowns them out.

The bleeding man sits there with his chest heaving and face swollen. He spits and curses at anyone dumb enough to pay him any attention.

The fan swirls above everything in slow motion, carrying with it the scent of death and failure from the people lying in beds that no one gives a fuck about. No one notices the dead leaving the room. They are motionless and silent underneath the sheets.

Another man sits in the corner, handcuffed to a chair, awaiting his fate but he already knows what's coming. I have seen him before. I have seen him often in my dreams. He is the key-holder to the morgue downtown. He is black as burned leather and with eyes a mixture of white and red. His smile reveals receded gums and rotten teeth. His skin is a stark contrast to the white shirt he wears and the blood red cowboy boots.

He grins at me and laughs to himself in a high-pitched giggle; the kind of laugh that tears at the fabric of sanity. He does not stop for the entire time we are there. You can hear his laughter down the hallway and out into the bay.

The janitor next to the man drags the mop across the floor endlessly into the morning and we all wait until the ritual is through. We all wait among the laughter and dried blood. We wait until we can walk away and forget the last few hours. We all wait until it starts again.

Bricks & Bones

I'm not sure what compelled me to do it – perhaps it was that small voice in the back of your mind – the one that tells you to do things in a reserved and cold tone. I could not have been older than eight – old enough to know right from wrong. I was told at an early age to defend myself as needed. My father insisted that I not allow myself to become a victim to bullying and up until that day I was unscathed. But what happened was something else entirely; it was something from deep inside that wanted to lash out and I would become all too familiar with it in the years to come.

When I was little my grandparents would babysit my brother and I while my mother took classes at the local University. They had a modest home in the suburbs and I have fond memories of that time. My cousin and I would play in my grandfather's camper or go to the nearby park. It was only when my cousin was not around that I would get into trouble.

Down the street, at the end of the cul-de-sac and next to the entrance to the park, lived an older boy whose name I cannot remember. I must have befriended him at some point but the only time I can ever remember seeing him is the time I almost killed him.

He was much larger than I was and in my memory, sinister looking – the way you would expect a bully to look – stocky, disheveled hair, a menacing grin on his face and lunch boxes for fists. I do not recall how it started but at some point he began to throw rocks and taunt me. I ran back to my grandparent's house, pelted the entire way by small stones. Some of them hit me in the legs and some in the back. With tears welled up in my eyes I remember the boy's shit-eating grin – he was enjoying himself immensely.

When we reached the house the rock-throwing stopped. He either grew bored with my torment or he was afraid of getting caught. Without saying a word I waited for him to turn his back to me. In my mind, I had already calculated an opportunity to exact my revenge – I knew, however, that it would only come were I patient. With insults still emitting from his crooked mouth he eventually started to walk back to his house.

My grandparent's home was flanked with red masonry bricks that were half-buried in the ground to serve as a border for the lawn. I saw that one of the bricks near my shoe was loose enough for me to pick it up. As he turned his back to me, confident that he had asserted himself (and probably already planning worse), I made my move. He lurched down the sidewalk, back to the safety of his home as I calmly and silently picked up the brick and walked after him.

The weight of the brick was impressive and it felt the way I expected it to: dangerous. Without saying a single word I hurled it with as much force as my body could create. It hit him squarely in the back just below his neck. I remember vividly the noise that forced its way from his throat. It was the kind of noise that a person makes when pain sends you reeling into the abyss of panic. It was not quite a scream but it was close enough – not all that different from the way a dog sounds the moment a car rolls over it.

He fell forward and crashed to the pavement in a giant and dull thud. I stood there for a moment watching – he was lifeless; a crumpled mass with blood pooling from underneath his head and running into the gutter.

I said absolutely nothing. I only looked on to see if he would twitch. He moaned at first and then began to wail and heave in deep breaths. I felt neither remorse nor a sense of urgency. I casually turned away, walked into the house and waited for the inevitable.

At that age I had no concept of the gravity of the situation. I knew that I would be in trouble but I also knew that the little bastard had it coming – he had pushed me too far. It was one of the earliest times I can remember being pushed to the edge and allowing instinct to take over.

What happened next is a blur of memory. I never saw the boy again. I walked past his home numerous times but we never crossed paths. I don't think I seriously injured him but that's beside the point.

I was punished and my grandparents talked at length about what to do with me. My grandmother was furious – she yelled and waved her hands around and said I would be lucky if the boy was ok and what the hell was the matter with me? Was I trying to kill him? Why did I not run for help and who gave me the idea?

My grandfather feigned anger but winked at me when my grandmother was not looking. "Good job, son," he said under his breath while he received the third degree about encouraging my behavior.

The truth is that no one gave me the idea. I simply reacted. My mind went blank and laid out a plan of action: hurt him. It satisfied something deep inside of me that I have only just begun to scratch the surface of.

The police were not involved and no one was sued. It was something that was never discussed again. I have thought about the boy over the years, always wondering what happened to him. Had the event changed him? Does he still think about it? I'll never know.

It would not be the last time I acted upon a violent instinct.

The Reverend Burns

There was strong wind blowing on the day it happened, bringing with it a touch of wickedness. It happened on the corner of nowhere and eternity on a busy street in Saigon; the kind of place where mean-spirited hookers sold false dreams on platform heels and slick prophet's silver tongues sought fat wallets.

It was on this day that the Reverend decided to make a statement that the world would remember. It was the summer season and the flowers in the trees were in full bloom; ripe with new seeds and ready to germinate. The streets of Saigon were themselves pregnant with violence, blood and desire. The hustle of sinners and collectors floated in the air like the wafting aroma of rotten flesh.

Women hurried down the street carrying heavy laundry and children while men of money went along in search of sin and sanctuary. The day was to be the most dramatic day of the New Year. It made sense to the Reverend that it would happen on this day; there was no freezing rain to contend with and no one was paying attention to much of anything other than the blood flowing along in the gutters.

The Reverend had planned things well.

The plan was simple; distract and move swiftly. Act simply and be not swayed by temptation. It was uncomplicated and direct; a parade under the watch of daylight and shadows would mask the real event. The Reverend knew that the hypnotic chant of the Buddhist Monks would drown out the sound of war and degeneration; they would turn no heads until it was too late.

And so on the morning on June 11 the yellow robed priests marched along in a single-file line of death. They had reached the world's stage with hardly anyone taking notice. Among them, almost hidden in their ranks, stepped forward a frail man in his sixties; a holy man glowing in yellow and white. The Reverend stepped forward and quietly assumed the lotus position on the street corner amidst the soldiers, the con men and whores.

Even as the moon was still visible in the morning sky, the monks moved with a grace and stealth as if under the cover of full darkness. The Reverend sat motionless as the others from the parade, the ones who had their faces masked in solemnity, proceeded to pour healthy amounts of gasoline on the old man as he sat and waited, expressionless and mute.

From across the busy road a little girl in the throes of horseplay with her brother paused and looked at the Reverend; their eyes locked in time while he smiled slowly. He reached into his yellow and flowing robe and removed a single match, its head igniting in slow motion as the little girl watched, mesmerized as everything surrounding them came to a complete stop.

No one breathed nor blinked. The cars and bikes in the street stood frozen as the women and the men waited and watched. Not a creature moved in that moment and there was nothing except the Reverend in full bloom of the season, fully and totally engulfed in flame.

And just as quickly as the silence had come over everyone, the moon was swallowed by the morning sky and the audience screamed in horror as the

Revered sat on the corner of nowhere and eternity, burning freely and as motionless as a statue.

The Reverend sat there in the lotus position for the entire world to see, on a stage of his making, resolute, with the smell of gasoline and burning flesh in the air. He sat like that for the rest of that day, for the rest of his life, forever more; burning his image into history.

His heart, the only part of the Reverend untouched by flame, was preserved and remains to this day an artifact and thing of legend. For on that day, the Reverend sacrificed his body so that his soul would live on and his face would imprint itself unto the clouds above.

Veteran of the Psychic Wars

I am tired. I am tired of reading the "news". I am tired of being plugged in and spoon fed empty rhetoric. I am tired of up-to-the-second updates. I'm tired of the mind games. I am tired of the wars. I am tired of being a suspect. I am tired of being the enemy.

I am tired of being coveted for my vote. I am tired of labels. I am tired of the contempt. I am tired of the apathy. I am tired of the hatred. I am tired of the race war. I am tired of the class war. I'm tired of politics. I'm tired of the fear.

I. Am. Tired.

I am tired of being divided and conquered. I am tired everyone wanting to be the same. I'm tired of sports entertainment. I am tired of political entertainment. I am tired of satire – both political and otherwise. I am tired of the television. I am tired of the Internet and the radio and internet radio.

I am tired of the non-stop, pornographic media gang bang that is obscenely repeated day after day. I am tired of worrying about winners and losers and I am tired of running to kick the proverbial football that is always pulled away at the last second.

I'm tired of social networking and I'm tired of non-stop advertising. I am tired of reading your bumper stickers. I am tired of hearing the opinions of strangers. I'm tired of eating bad and I am tired of feeling bad about eating bad.

I'm tired of watching the clock and tired of worrying about how much time is left. I'm tired of being told what to think and who to root for. I'm tired of the lies. I'm tired of second guesses and I'm tired of questions without answers. I'm tired of the insanity and of the rallies to restore sanity.

I am tired of the government sanctioned book burnings and Satanic politicians. I am tired of government hit lists that are sponsored by mega-corporations. I am tired of the united states of corporations. I am tired of the push to dumb everything down. I'm tired of being told this is a democracy and or republic. I'm tired of being told my voice counts. I am tired of the two-party system and I am tired of the same old contest between a giant douche and a turd sandwich.

How long exactly before we're all together in a packed theater laughing hysterically at a two-hour film consisting of nothing more than an ass farting?

I am tired of the war on terror, the war on bacon, the war on drugs, the war on freedom, the war on [insert asinine corporate holiday here], the war on napkins, the war on brown people, the war on war and the war on the color blue. War!!

I am tired of book banning, parents fretting, old people upsetting and the absence of higher learning. I am tired of the national Deport-A-Thon and the never-ending search for the Tacos of Mass Destruction.

Fuck it.

I'm offended, you're offended, Mama we're all offended now. I am tired of the fear of a Brown planet and the fear of a gay planet. Fear, fear, fear!!!

Puppets, Muppets and pundits – I am so very goddamned tired of it all.

I would like to invoke Tim Leary and drop out – right off of the goddamned grid if I could and into total oblivion with a good song, a good book and an appetite for destruction. I never had any faith to begin with and have even less now.

I am a veteran – nothing more, nothing less.

These wars that we have waged will go on and on and I will remain where I always have – on the edge and unsure if there's anything left fighting for except my family.

Redneck Zen

Patrick Swayze died the other day and for a moment I remembered all of my favorite Swayze lines from his films that I liked. Swayze was often the same character in his movies – a spiritual tough guy with a dry sense of humor. His on-screen persona burned itself into the minds of many movie-goers over the years; he was either Dalton, Darry, Bodhi or Johnny (the dancing guy). I always liked his role as Derek Sutton, a minor league hockey tough guy in Youngblood. I would be lying if I declined to admit that Point Break is one of my all-time favorite movies, not because it's good, but because it has so many great lines in it.

When Swayze died my thoughts did not linger on the man's work for long but instead turned to some of his fans and their obsessions with his movies. I've met a few in my time but I immediately thought of Harry, a slob I used to work with in Emergency Services.

Harry (not his real name) was a lonely fat guy who answered phones for a living in the middle of the night. Wherever a local grandma fell out of bed and broke her hip, Harry answered her call. Wherever a nurse wanted to push her dying patient off on the local emergency room, Harry was there…on the phone.

Wherever Walgreens was having a 3:00 A.M. sale on frozen pizza, Harry was there.

Harry was an overnight emergency dispatcher with zero social skills. When people called for help, he answered the phone and sent us screaming down the road, our apathy in tow. He was not particularly skilled at his job and he could have cared less about anyone other than himself. To this day I have no idea how anyone understood half of what he said as he always had food in his mouth. "Man down, chest pain" sounded more like "mah mown, spess meh".

Everyone hated Harry. He had a poor disposition and little common sense. He was piggish, rude and overbearing. It was not a good idea to get on his bad side either as he would have you out all night answering calls for "distress" from phone booths on Main Street.

Harry's least redeeming quality however, was his obsession with the Patrick Swayze film, Roadhouse. When I first met him, I did not consciously notice that whenever I walked into the dispatch office, Roadhouse was on. It did not matter what day of the week it was or what time of the night – Dalton was always kicking someone's ass. Harry worked 12-hour shifts in spans of two days on and two days off. In a single shift, he could watch the film six times…and sometimes, he did.

To each his own, right…? I could never, for the life of me, figure out what the obsession was about…though I had an idea. Everyone did. Harry did not just have your run of the mill, taped-from cable copy of Roadhouse, no – he had the real thing: uncensored, un-cut and with all the soft-core porn restored to its original form.

You could write a doctoral thesis on Roadhouse and its tangled web of social commentary. It is a film that defies logic yet has a cult following unlike any other film. Armchair philosophers can wax poetic on the lone-wolf character Dalton and his struggle against…well, that is up to interpretation. The point is, Roadhouse has a philosophy and its characters thinly veiled substance. It is Redneck zen.

On a busy night Harry would be left in the dispatch office by himself for hours at a time. We would find ourselves on the corner of Rape and Carjack, answering a call for "my foot hurts so I need pain meds" only to ask dispatch why the hell he took the bogus call in the first place.

It became obvious that Harry relished his "alone time" with Dalton and the girls of the Double Deuce. Not only was he touching himself to Roadhouse but he was doing it multiple times a night, every night. It was creepy on a level difficult to put into words.

One fateful night, my partner and I decided to hijack Harry's copy of his favorite movie as a joke. We planned to keep it for a couple of shifts to see what his reaction would be. Would he have a meltdown? Go postal? Call the police? We didn't know.

A page came through asking all available units to be on the lookout for his copy of the movie. Then he repeated his request over the radio…with the F.C.C. listening.

We had a good laugh the rest of the shift and got our asses handed to us by Harry, who was obviously disgruntled without his obsession. The night turned into day and I did not think about it until the next shift.

Much to my surprise, when I arrived at work the next day, I discovered Harry watching Roadhouse. I looked at my partner, whom I was sure had given him the movie back but I was wrong. Harry brought in a back-up copy of the movie…

To this day I do not know which is worse; that Harry spent most of his waking hours masturbating to a Patrick Swayze film or that he had emergency copies of said film. I never bothered to ask. Life went on until Harry was fired for reasons unknown. Some attributed it to his "hobby" and I am sure that is not far from the truth. He was a strange person to say the least. I have never seen someone obsess over a film as much as he did.

The last I heard, Harry was driving a cab somewhere in the city. He is without his precious movie (we never gave it back) and without the luxury of privacy. I am sure the news of Swayze's death hit him hard but who knows? I am also sure Dalton lives on forever in the minds of those who put him on a pedestal of barroom brawls, naked, outdoor tai-chi and sex in public bathrooms. Harry is someone you will never meet and for that, consider yourself lucky.

Elvis, Sin City and the Prosthetic Leg

We have to go back to Sin City. I hate going to Sin City. It's like a circus for the criminally insane. You see things there that are not normal; it's like insanity in slow motion only it's narrated by you. If the whole world is a stage then these are some seriously fucked up players.

It's 100-degrees outside with the kind of humidity that kills old people. Most of the people that live here are F4L (Fucked-4-Life). Many of them look like runners-up in the annual Charles Manson look-a-like contest…if Charles was brain dead and suffering from Aids and post-traumatic stress disorder.

There is a little old Black lady that sits out front next to the statue of green-rusted Jesus. The sign underneath him says: "all are welcome in His kingdom". If this is God's kingdom, I'll pass.

The Black lady has the 1,000-yard stare and says the exact same phrase over and over and over…while clapping her tiny hands together in the air like a hummingbird's wings

"Ple-ase, lord! Ple-ase, lord! Ple-ase, lord! Ple-ase, lord! Ple-ase, lord! Ple-ase, lord! Ple-ase lord! Ple-ase, lord!"

Wheeling the stretcher through the automatic doors the scenery is right out of Jacob's Ladder, complete with disfigured midgets and convulsing, screaming people strapped to chairs. The smell is a mixture of curdled milk and shit with piss-stained sheets and vomit mixed in for good measure. And of course, there is the scent of death in the air to contend with.

On this particular day an Elvis impersonator is performing for the horde of Charles Manson look-a-likes. He's a big fat guy wearing a blue - sequined costume with tassels and white cowboy boots. He has more gel in his hair that I have ever used in my entire life. It looks like motor oil. He's singing

"A Big Hunk o' Love" and doing a really bad job of it. He can hardly breathe and you can hear him gasp for air between verses. No one notices. I'm not quite sure his audience is even breathing. That would be funny: a whole room full of dead people being serenaded by fat Elvis. Maybe not.

The floors are dirty and my unzipped boots stick to the tile. I have to wonder what I am stepping on. Of course the nurse does not speak English and her henchmen are too brain dead to be of any help. So it's a big guessing game again.

Our patient's mother is in the room. She is hovering over him, audibly praying to "the Lord" and fumble-fucking with his prosthetic leg, which is now coated with piss. No matter how hard she tries she just can't seem to get it back on her son's stump. There isn't a nurse to be found. The patient is flailing and thrashing around on the bed and I'm staring at my partner because: a.) we haven't eaten lunch and b.) they don't pay us enough money to deal with this kind of shit by ourselves.

"Hey baby, I ain't askin' much of you

No no no no no no no no baby, I ain't askin' much of you

Just a big-a big-a hunk o' love will do…"

After prying the guy's mother off of him and tipping over a bucket of piss we manage to load the guy on the stretcher and make a break for the ambulance. His mother makes it a point to stuff the plastic leg on top of him as we go – never mind that I am bagging him or that his heart rhythm looks like shit.

"Don't be cruel…

to a heart that's true…"

And right as we pass by the Elvis extravaganza on the way out the guy codes.

The end.

About the Author

S. J. Rivera is a Xicano writer, indie publisher and stranger in a strange land. Originally from Denver, Colorado, Rivera now calls Northeast, Florida home. He is the author of **Demon in the Mirror** and **Alcohol Soaked & Nicotine Stained**. Rivera made his bones as a journalist, EMT and independent publisher. He has performed spoken word in several unknown coffee shops and on street corners from the Rocky Mountains to the mean streets of the Dirty South.

Broken Sword Publications